The Loved One

The Loved One

CATHERINE PALMER
PEGGY STOKS

Tyndale House Publishers
WHEATON, ILLINOIS

Visit Tyndale's exciting Web site at www.tyndale.com

Edited by Kathryn S. Olson

Designed by Ron Kaufmann

Some Scripture quotations are taken from the *Holy Bible,* King James Version.

Some Scripture quotations are taken from the *Holy Bible,* New Living Translation, copyright © 1996. Used by permission of Tyndale House Publishers, Inc., Wheaton, Illinois 60189. All rights reserved.

This novel is a work of fiction. Names, characters, places, and incidents are either the product of the authors' imaginations or are used fictitiously. Any resemblance to actual events, locales, organizations, or persons living or dead is entirely coincidental and beyond the intent of either the authors or publisher.

Library of Congress Cataloging-in-Publication Data

Palmer, Catherine, date.
  The loved one / Catherine Palmer and Peggy Stoks.
    p. cm. — (Moving fiction)
  ISBN 0-8423-7214-8 (hc)
    1. Soldiers—Family relationships—Fiction. 2. Vietnamese Conflict, 1961-1975—
Veterans—Fiction. 3. Recruiting and enlistment—Fiction. 4. Mothers and sons—Fiction.
I. Stoks, Peggy. II. Title. III. Series.

PS3566.A495 L677 2003
813′.54—dc21   2003004994

Printed in the United States of America

09 08 07 06 05 04 03
9   8   7   6   5   4   3   2

To those who serve

The greatest love is shown
when people lay down their lives for their friends.
You are My friends if you obey Me.

JOHN 15:13-14, NLT

Acknowledgments

I am deeply grateful to Lori Copeland, who has been my friend and mentor for many years. While on a book-promotion tour to St. Joseph, Missouri, Lori suggested that she and I collaborate on a story. Walking through the Pony Express Museum, we excitedly plotted *The Loved One*.

I was sorry to learn a few weeks later that Lori's busy writing schedule would prevent her from participating in the project. Lori graciously gave her permission for another dear friend, Peggy Stoks, to write the book with me. Thank you, Lori, and let's try again!

—CATHERINE PALMER

I am grateful for the assistance of former Army officer Vince Junker, whose knowledge of military history can be described in no other way than amazing. His assistance in helping me find suitable battles in which to set my stories was invaluable, as was his continued help in proofreading each of the four vignettes that appear in *The Loved One*.

For special assistance regarding the American Revolution I want to acknowledge Michael and Sonja Meals. I found them through their Web site, www.revwar.com, and they graciously answered my many questions about the American

Revolution and later proofread Deborah Chilton's story. Dairy farmer Don Alberts is also to be thanked for patiently answering my questions about rural life.

Dr. Daniel Stowell, director and editor of *The Papers of Abraham Lincoln,* couldn't have been more generous or gracious in assisting me with Elizabeth Chilton's story. His comments and suggestions, along with those of his colleague Dr. Glenna Schroeder-Lein, were extremely helpful. I also want to thank Tom Schwartz, Illinois State Historian and Secretary of the Abraham Lincoln Association, for providing the resources he did.

The Circle Pines librarians came through with a magnificent number of interlibrary loans for this project. For their continued helpfulness and encouragement with each of my projects, I want them to know how deeply they are appreciated.

Finally, a great big *merci beaucoup* to Char Swanson and Maureen Pratt for their assistance in helping me use the French language. The more French I learn, the more I realize how much I have yet to learn. *Eh, bien . . .*

— PEGGY STOKS

Chilton Family Genealogy

Caleb Chilton *m* Elizabeth
(came to Plymouth in 1630 as a small boy)
David

David Chilton – b. 1649, d. 1690
m Mary Whipple, daughter of Captain Isaac Whipple
Elijah

Elijah Chilton – b. 1688, d. 1749, *m* Mercy
Zebulon (at least two brothers)

Zebulon Chilton – b. 5/2/1719, d. ?
m Hannah Coleman – b. 1730?, d. ?
Paul, Lemuel

Paul Chilton – b. 4/5/1749, d. 10/16/1811
m Deborah Easterbrook – b. 6/20/1753, d. 9/4/1812
Theodore (d. at birth), Samuel, Caleb, Hiram, Luke, Dorcas, Peter, Ruth, Rachel

Samuel Chilton – b. 1780, d. ?, *m* Polly White – b. ?, d. ?
Arabella, Prudence, Honora, Hettie, Theodore

Theodore Chilton – b. 10/4/1809, d. 2/12/1879
m Sophiea Preston – b. 1/1809 or 1/1810, d. 9/4/1872
Stephen, Alice, Lydia (d. of pneumonia), Alden, Lyman, Levi, Olive, Eli

Alden Eugene Chilton – b. 7/20/1836, d. ?
m Elizabeth Rogers – b. 9/30/1838, d. 8/16/1908
Ellen, Mary (d. in childhood), Bertha and Oscar (twins),
Lucia (d. at birth), Arthur

Oscar F. Chilton – b. 6/13/1875, d. 10/21/1916
m Cornelia Vogt – b. 2/24/1878, d. 8/22/1945
Henry Alden, Willis John

Willis John Chilton – b. 4/1/1899, d. 1/26/1964
m Lorna Mae McConnell Chilton – b. 10/10/1902, d. 9/27/1988
(widow of Henry Chilton)
Pearl Irene (fathered by Henry),
Mabel Rose (fathered by Henry), Irving Kent, Donald Joseph

Irving Kent Chilton – b. 5/14/1925, d. 8/6/1980
m Solange Marie Nadal – b. 6/19/1926, d. 1/25/2004
Jacob, Daniel

Daniel Edward Chilton – b. 11/12/1954
m Margaret (Meg) Stark – b. 9/6/1957
Tyler John Chilton

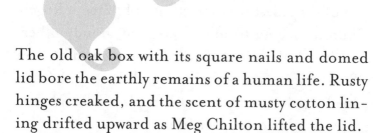

The old oak box with its square nails and domed
lid bore the earthly remains of a human life. Rusty
hinges creaked, and the scent of musty cotton lin-
ing drifted upward as Meg Chilton lifted the lid.

But this was no casket. Inside the small, hand-
crafted chest lay a tarnished silver locket and a yellowed envelope. They were all that remained of
Deborah Chilton, a woman whose blood now flowed
through the veins of Meg's only child.

She set the box on her large desk amid the array
of memorabilia gathered there. Determined to
provide her son with a meaningful gift for his high
school graduation, she had spent her evenings dur-

ing the past four years compiling a detailed genealogical record of the family.

At the back of the desk, a stack of history books and biographies rose to a precarious height. Beside the books, Meg had arranged the precious few photographs she had been able to obtain—faded and sepia-toned images of men in Army uniforms, babies propped on blankets, and brides and grooms standing solemnly side by side. Her favorite, and one of the oldest, was a portrait of Elizabeth Rogers Chilton, her husband's great-great-grandmother, clad in a full-skirted, Civil War—era gown of dark silk with white lace at the neck and sleeves. Meg had added a pale blue mat and had placed the photograph in an ornate silver frame.

On the other side of her desk lay old photograph albums, a set of love letters tied with a red ribbon, and several marriage licenses and military documents. During her years of research, Meg had penned a detailed journal about each member of the Chilton family. In the leather-bound notebook, she recorded tidbits of oral history that had filtered down through the generations, comments from passing historians, and data taken from old diaries and letters. Gradually, she had compiled biographies—some of them far too short, she thought—that helped to flesh out the lives of her son's ancestors. This journal, this record of his heritage, would be her graduation gift to Tyler John Chilton.

But until today, when her husband brought his mother's small jewelry box from Solange Chilton's attic, Meg had been stalled at the Revolutionary War. Her chart included men's names, of course, and a few anecdotes about those who had fought in various battles. But the women—particularly Deborah Chilton—remained a mystery. Meg knew neither birth nor death dates, nothing about her life, not even the woman's maiden name. Eager to study the chest's contents, she reached for the locket.

Her hand paused as Meg caught the familiar sounds of her son's sneakers clomping across the wooden floor downstairs, his letter jacket dropping on the couch, and his backpack flopping onto the kitchen table. She stepped to the door of her home office, where she worked as a freelance designer. "Hey, Tyler, you've got to see this! Your dad found an old jewelry box in *Grandmaman* Solange's attic."

"Just a minute, Mom." Tyler's husky voice filtered upstairs. Its deep timbre still sometimes took his mother by surprise. "I gotta eat something first. I'm starving."

"This dates all the way back to the Revolutionary War!"

"Hey, don't we have any Little Debbies?"

"Look in the pantry."

Meg sighed and returned to the box. She found it frustrating that despite her enthusiasm, neither her husband nor their son shared her passion for genealogy. Her own history had been almost too easy to track—both parents had immigrated to the United States from Norway, and their records were preserved in church archives. But Dan Chilton's family tree grew this way and that, a winding, twisting mass of branches and fruit. Nearly every ethnic group in America's melting pot played some role in the Chilton history.

"Where in the pantry?" Tyler called up.

"By the Cheerios!"

How could a boy be a senior in high school, a four-year honor roll student, a National Merit finalist, a track star, and a scholarship winner bound for Yale University—and still not remember where his mom kept the snacks?

"I don't see 'em," he hollered.

"Third shelf down, on the left. Paper towels, soups, Cheerios, Little Debbies."

"Got it!"

Meg closed her eyes. Now Tyler would be taking a large glass from the cabinet and pouring milk to its brim. He would peel back the clear wrapping from the Devil Squares and stuff half of one cake into his mouth. Without chewing or swallowing, he would pour in a mouthful of cold milk. And then, his cheeks bulging, he would devour this bite in the space of about three seconds. Would any other Yale freshmen eat like that despite *their* mothers' best efforts?

Shaking her head, Meg pinched the silver locket chain between her thumb and forefinger and gingerly lifted the oval necklace from the jewelry box. All these years she'd been trying to find out about Deborah Chilton, the woman whose bloodline could be traced through eight generations from the Revolutionary War. Then Dan's mother had passed away at age seventy-seven. Finally, there amid the clutter in *Grandmaman* Solange's dusty attic, he had found it—the legendary family heirloom that had vanished for three generations.

Slipping her fingernail into the tiny groove on the side of the locket, Meg pried open the two halves. A shiver skittered down her spine as she gazed on the painted miniature of a beautiful woman. Her dark hair was swept up in a knot, and her depthless blue eyes stared forward. It was a rough portrait, no doubt executed by an itinerant artist, but it captured the determined spirit of the woman.

"What're we having for supper?" Tyler called up.

"There's a roast in the Crock-Pot."

"Roast?"

"It's right there on the counter." Blind, Meg thought, the boy was blind. "Hey, come up here and look at this, Tyler. It's amazing. I'm holding a picture of your ancestor from eight generations ago."

"Just a sec. I gotta call Charlie, see what he's doing tonight. We might order a pizza."

"Tyler, I am cooking a roast!" Was he deaf too? "You can invite Charlie for dinner. There's plenty."

Silence. Meg pried open the silver panel that covered the other half of the locket. A small curl of dark hair tied with a white ribbon slipped out onto her lap.

"Oh, Tyler, it's her hair!" she cried. "They saved her hair!"

"Huh?"

"Your great-great-great-great-great-great-grandmother's hair! I'm holding it."

"Yuck."

"Tyler, get up here right now!"

"Okay, okay."

Meg set the locket aside and picked up the old envelope. On the front someone had written: "Deborah Easterbrook Chilton. Born June 20, 1753. Died September 4, 1812."

Easterbrook. That was the maiden name she'd been seeking!

Tingling with excitement, Meg realized this was absolutely invaluable. She glanced up at the long row of pages she had tacked to the wall of her office. At last, she would be able to fill in the blank at the far end of the genealogical chart.

She turned the envelope over and read another notation: "Deborah Easterbrook Chilton. Played important role in Rv. War."

An important role? Meg's heart began to thud. *Grandmaman* Solange had mentioned the old box, the locket, and the ancestor who had brought the family line from England. But there had been no mention of any role the woman might have played in the struggle for independence.

"Tyler, she was a war hero!" Meg looked up as her son emerged from the stairwell. The trace of a milk mustache clung to the wispy tendrils on his unshaven upper lip. She carried the locket to him. "Look at this picture. Isn't she pretty? Her name was Deborah Easterbrook Chilton, and the inscription on the back of this envelope says she played a key role in the Revolutionary War."

"Cool." He studied the locket for a moment. "Why's her hair in there? That's gross."

"That's what they used to do in memory of a loved one."

"Don't ever do that to me. Just shut the coffin and let me go."

"Tyler, that's morbid."

"Keeping some dead lady's hair is morbid."

"This was not 'some dead lady.' She's your great-great-great-great-great-great-grandmother. Look at this stuff." He followed her to the cluttered desk. "Can you believe this was in *Grandmaman* Solange's attic all along? See, my chart stops right here. I got this far with the Chiltons, and then I ran into a dead end. I didn't have her maiden name or anything. You know, you can't go hopping back to England if you don't have the right connections. There were lots of Chiltons in pre-Revolutionary War America, believe me. I had no birth or death dates to put in this space either. Nothing. But now that I know the name and the dates, I can fill in the blank. Deborah Easterbrook Chilton—and look, she had black hair and blue eyes, just like you. Isn't that amazing?"

She turned to find her son standing by the window and gazing down at the street below. Tall and lanky, he leaned one shoulder against the frame and traced the wooden mullions that divided the windowpanes. Stricken anew with the imminent absence of her son—his graduation in two weeks, his summer job at a Christian camp, and then his four years at college—Meg felt her stomach churn. She knew it was time to let him go. Time for him to test those wings he'd been growing and strengthening all these years. Time for him to fly away into his own life. But, oh, it was going to be quiet around the house. Quiet, empty . . . lonely.

"You okay, Tyler?" she asked softly.

His focus darted to her face. "Mom, I need to talk to you about something."

"Sure. Anything." She perched on the corner of her desk, affecting a casual pose. How many times had he made such an announcement—and how many times had she feigned calm and serenity? She could almost hear the roll call of incidents that began with "Mom, I need to talk to you about something. . . ." *I fell off the slide today and cut my knee open; I punched Johnny in the nose for calling me a nerd; I made a D on my art project; I'm going out with Amber; Amber dumped me; I'm dropping an elective; I'm going out with Shelley; I dumped Shelley. . . .* On and on . . .

As always, Tyler flushed a pale shade of pink and rubbed his palms on his blue-jean-clad thighs. As always, he cleared his throat and swallowed a few times. As always, he seemed to search too long for the right words. And then he spoke.

"Mom, I've decided not to go to Yale in the fall," he said quickly. "I've been praying a long time about this, and I talked it over with my youth pastor—and I feel like God's telling me to enlist in the military. Army. I'm supposed to protect our country."

Meg stared at her son as the blood drained out of her head. Not go to Yale? Not accept a full scholarship to the finest university in the nation? Not compete on its track team?

A soldier?

Every droplet of protective mother-tiger instinct rose up inside Meg to form a gigantic wave of determination. "No," she said. "Absolutely not."

"What?"

"I said no. Tyler, that's not possible. You're going to Yale and get yourself a great education and have a wonderful, fulfilling life. You are not joining the Army."

He straightened from the window. Breathing hard, he clenched his jaw and glared at her. "Mom, you don't understand."

"Who put this idea into your head?" she demanded, determined to ferret out and punish the perpetrator.

"Nobody!" He paused. "That's not what I mean. It was God. He showed me this."

"How?"

"Well, I got to thinking about all the things that have been happening to our country—the threats, the attempts at sabotage, the attacks. It's not right. Someone has to defend the people of the United States, and I believe it should be me. I watch you and Dad, Uncle Jake and Aunt Martha, the kids in the playground near the high school track, even the girl who works the counter at the Dairy Queen—"

"Is this about a girl, Tyler?"

"No, Mom, I'm trying to tell you that I watch these people—most of them I don't even know—and I think about their futures. I care about their lives. I want to protect them from harm. Dad fought in Vietnam, and you've told me about other Chiltons who were military men. Now it's my turn. I've been praying about this for a long time. I feel like it's what God wants me to do, Mom."

"God gave you a scholarship to Yale, Tyler. What on earth would make you think He wants you to enlist in the Army?"

"I can't explain it. It's just something I know. It's like a sense of determination that's really strong inside my heart—and you always told me to search my heart. So I did, and this is what I'm supposed to do."

"But enlist? You mean go to boot camp and then be sent straight off to an Army base somewhere? If you're so determined to join the military, why don't you become an officer? You're smart enough for that. Be in the ROTC while you're at Yale. Or join the Air Force—go to the academy in Colorado."

"No, Mom. I plan to enlist in the regular Army. I can't afford to take the time for officer training or the Air Force Academy. I need to do this, don't you see? I feel called to take action. Right now."

"Have you discussed this with your father?"

"Not yet, but I know he'll be okay with it. He's told me about Vietnam, and he—"

"And he nearly died of malaria in some make-shift medic tent out in the steaming jungle! There's more than bullets or grenades that can kill you on a battlefield, Tyler." Hot tears flooded her eyes as she thought of the suffering her husband had endured all those years ago. He had been so young, so sick, and so alone. "Our enemies are using chemicals now, and biological weapons."

"I know, and they have to be stopped."

"But you could be wounded trying to stop those people. Horribly scarred. You could be disabled by a land mine, Tyler. Have you thought about living the rest of your life without your legs? You're a track star! You could lose your arms, too, or your eyesight or your hearing. And it's not just physical scarring I'm talking about. Walk down any big-city street, and you're going to see mentally ill, homeless people—many of them veterans. Vietnam veterans came back with terrible trauma. Post-traumatic stress syndrome, suicidal depression, even schizophrenia. War does terrible things to people, Tyler. Some become drug addicts. They live under bridges."

"Mom, I'm a Christian. I have high moral standards. You know that."

"Yes, but the military is very different from the church youth group, believe me. You wouldn't have that kind of support, and you wouldn't be able to call your youth pastor to ask his advice. How can you be sure you wouldn't stray from the Lord, honey? The temptations out there are so great—alcohol, prostitution, drugs. And when you're off in some foreign country alone and frightened—"

"You rely on God's strength, not your own. I'll face those same temptations when I go to college,

Mom. And I could die at Yale just as easily as on a battlefield. I could step off a curb and get hit by a—"

"Not just as easily! I know you'll encounter temptations at college, and I realize life is fragile. But you're telling me you want to throw yourself right square in the path of every physical, emotional, and spiritual danger there is."

Tyler gazed at her, his eyes unflinching. "Mom, I'm going to join the Army. I've made up my mind. But I want your blessing. Can I have it?"

"No," Meg snapped as a tear spilled down her cheek. "You cannot go into the military and fight and get wounded or killed! I won't allow it."

"So, I don't have your blessing?" He looked like a five-year-old, disappointed and confused.

"No."

"Mom, you and Dad brought me up in church. You've read to me from the Bible every single day of my life. You taught me what it means to be a Christian and how to follow God's leading. It was through your example that I gave my life to Christ. You're the one who told me over and over again to seek God's will and to do whatever He asks."

"Yes, but not this, Tyler!"

"Mom, it shouldn't matter *what*. It should only matter that I say yes. And I've said yes. This is what I'm supposed to do. Please give me your blessing!"

Meg brushed the tear from her cheek as the image of military coffins being unloaded from the belly of a plane flashed through her mind. She saw night skies with screaming antiaircraft fire streaking through the blackness. She saw the hollow eyes of the sick and wounded. She saw body bags, rows of the dead lined up for burial.

"Tyler," she whispered, "you are my only child. You're the precious bone of my bone and flesh of my flesh. You're the son for whom I prayed night and day for too many years to count. And when your dad and I had abandoned all hope of ever having children—God chose to bless us with a baby boy. You're a miracle, Tyler. You're all I have."

"So it's only moms with lots of kids who should send their sons or daughters to war?" Tyler was staring at her, resentment filling his blue eyes. "Is that what you're saying, Mom? If a woman has two sons, then she can send one of them to battle—like his place could ever be filled by the other one?

Mom, there's no such thing as a *spare* kid. Each child is special."

"Yes, and you're *my* special child. You're my only son, and I will never give you my blessing to enlist."

His lip trembled as he leveled a dark gaze at her. "Charlie and I are going out for pizza and a movie. I'll be back around eleven."

"Okay," she said, closing her eyes as her son brushed past her. "I'll wait up."

She heard the echo of his shoes pounding down the stairs and the slam of the back screen door. And then she heard his car's engine roar to life.

Sinking into the chair at her desk, Meg laid her hand on the old box. A tuft of hair, a tiny portrait. This was all that remained of Deborah Chilton. This was what death left behind. This was the nothingness, the emptiness that followed in its wake.

She wanted more than this for her son. Much more.

Meg picked up the envelope again. No woman of good conscience would willingly risk the life of her only child, she thought as she shook the envelope and a small, folded newspaper clipping fell into her hand. It was a woman's duty to love and protect her offspring, and no military or political cause could possibly be great enough to lead her to willingly sacrifice that loved one.

Certain she had taken the right stand in refusing to bless her son's decision, Meg opened the faded yellow paper and scanned the article. "Cemetery Holds Grave of Revolutionary War Hero: A Woman" the headline read. It was dated July 1, 1936:

Deborah Chilton's grave in New Hope Cemetery was rediscovered Thursday by Cornelia Vogt Chilton, president of the town's Ladies Society. Cornelia was touring the site with other members of the organization. Deborah Chilton is remembered as a heroine for her role in aiding American colonists in their struggle against the tyranny of King George III and his Redcoats . . . .

New York
September 1777

The western sky gleamed red-gold as Deborah Chilton walked from the house to the barn. In her hand swung the milk pail, still dripping from its washing. After a day of hard labor, both indoors and out, the fresh, chill air of twilight was a welcome refreshment against her heated face. Her aching back and legs yearned for the comfort of bed, but the cows needed milking, the horse expected its grain, and the chickens had to be shut in their coop.

Nonetheless, I choose to be thankful, she told herself, feeling the babe stir in her womb. After five years of barrenness, she was amazed and overjoyed that God had granted her the blessing of motherhood, one of the deepest desires of her heart. Only two months remained until the birth of this much-hoped-for child.

Her husband, Paul, who first had been called as part of the militia, then later commissioned captain, promised he would do everything in his power to be granted a furlough in late autumn. But times were uncertain, and Deborah did not know of his company's whereabouts. Some days she missed him so much that she carried an actual physical ache inside her. But she clung to the hope and promise of their coming child, to lasting victory for the Patriots, and to independence for this beautiful land. And, always, she clung to her faith.

A tangy mixture of aromas tickled her nose when she stepped across the threshold into the barn. Paul had built the structure with his own hands, setting the building on a handsome stone foundation. Though emptier of hay and grain than in autumns past, the barn was snug and tight. If she managed carefully, she should be able to nourish the stock through the coming winter.

"Coming, old girl," Deborah replied to Daisy's impatient mooing. Her eyes adjusted to the dimness as she set down the pail and took the milking stool from the shelf. She hummed a little, anticipating how pleasant it would be to sit for a short spell. Soon Daisy's milk was zinging into the bucket. As was Deborah's habit while milking, she prayed for the safety of her husband and her two brothers, all of whom had taken up arms for the Patriot cause.

The unmistakable sound of a human cough sent alarm coursing through Deborah's veins. There were more than a few Loyalists in these parts, but thus far she had been spared trouble by the British, who were encamped much closer than she would like. After hearing the dreadful stories of Lord Cornwallis's troops' plundering, she worried about suffering the same fate as New Jersey's hapless residents. Homes, livestock, mills, and orchards had been destroyed; women violated by the score.

"Hullo? Who's there?" she demanded to know, rising to glance at the doorway. Paul had left her a pair of pistols, but they were at the house. Helplessly, she realized the axe was at the woodpile, waiting to be put away.

The sickle?

There was no one in the doorway, so she moved with ungainly haste to the wall and removed the heavy, curve-bladed instrument. "I will not hesitate to defend my farm," she declared, fear sharpening her senses.

For a long, tense moment, nothing was heard

but the sounds of the barn. Daisy mooed her displeasure at a job only half done and stamped her hoof. Deborah swallowed, realizing it soon would be too dark to see anything at all. Who was about, and what did he want? Dare she light the candle? Her grip on the sickle handle grew slick, and she nearly dropped the blade at the rasp of a hoarse voice.

"I mean you no harm."

"Who are you? *Where* are you?" she demanded again, taking a cautious step toward the rear of the barn, from whence she believed the voice came. "I'll thank you to rid yourself of my barn and be on your way."

"I . . . can't."

"Why so?"

"I'm hurt, missus."

"You're alone?"

"If there is no one else about, then I am alone. But I bring you warning that Burgoyne is on the move. You may not be safe."

"Rumor and false information abound. Why should I believe you?"

"Because . . ." His voice trailed off, ending in a

grunt of pain. "I suppose you are a woman alone. Is there a trustworthy American man about?"

"Every trustworthy American man of these parts has been raised to bear arms against the British, my husband included. But you find a fair number who display the white-paper badge of Loyalist."

"Is there not one dependable American?" asked the man, his voice stretched with pain and desperation.

Something about the question made Deborah's grip loosen, and she set the sickle down while she lit the candle. Once the flame flickered and caught, she retrieved her weapon and moved cautiously toward the rear of the barn. Most likely the man had found refuge behind the tall haystack there.

Her breath caught in her throat when she noticed the great, dark stains on the floor. So he had come in through the back, through the pasture entrance. Though she was yet to be fully convinced of his loyalty, she had no doubt of his injury.

"Sir, I am coming toward you. I can see you are badly wounded." Rounding the haystack, she was struck by the sight of a dark-haired man who appeared to be in his mid-twenties. His face was pinched with pain. His shirt and jacket were a ghastly mess of blood, and his hands were cupped over his abdomen, working in vain to stanch the flow of deep red that seeped between his fingers.

When his gaze met hers, she saw resignation. "Lucky shot for the British . . . but no more luck for me." He worked hard to swallow. "Seems I have no . . . choice."

"What are you saying?" Setting aside the sickle, Deborah knelt down on one knee, her heart overcome with pity.

He inclined his head, ever so slightly, to the right. "The packet. Intelligence for General Gates . . . must get through." A spasm of pain gripped him then, leaving him panting and agitated as it abated. "Promise me you'll find some-one—tonight! Promise!"

"You have my word," Deborah replied, alarmed at his manner and at the shuddering which now overtook him. "At the very least, will you tell me your name?"

"J-John. John Kilby."

"John, I'll leave you the candle while I go for some rags and warm water—"

"No." Unexpectedly, his arm snaked out and caught her wrist, making her gasp. "No," he said again, more weakly, his grip loosening, then sliding away. "I must tell you . . . some things."

A sob caught in Deborah's throat as she set down the candle. Her fingers fumbled to untie her apron, and she folded it hastily, inside out, pressing its cleanest side over his wound. She took one of his hands in hers, unmindful of its bloodiness; with her other hand she smoothed the hair from his brow. His face was ghostly pale in the candlelight, his eyes deep and glassy.

In irregular speech, he gave her the location of the British, the route he believed the next courier should take, and the password that would admit the rider to the Continental camp.

Deborah concentrated on John's words, memorizing every bit of the critical information. Though an idea was beginning to take shape in her mind, she did not speak of it aloud. Her heart pounded as he added, "Choose your man well. He should be reliable . . . courageous . . . and clever."

In halting phrases, he told her how he'd come upon a British foraging party, quite by surprise.

Though the enemy were having their noon meal, their mounts tied some distance from the fire, one man had stood and gotten off a shot that pierced the Patriot's belly. Wheeling his horse about, John made his escape. After a long, painful ride, he had turned his horse loose, then taken refuge in the Chilton cornfield until he was satisfied he had not been followed. Slowly, he'd made his way into the barn.

"How I prayed you weren't Tory," he whispered, closing his eyes.

"Chiltons are anything but." Fierceness rose inside Deborah as she studied the face of the wounded courier, his complexion having taken on a waxy pallor during the short time they'd talked. Death was near. It struck her that her husband or one of her brothers might one day be in similar circumstances, far from home and among strangers or enemies, if anyone at all. This soldier, John, who fought so valiantly against the tyranny of the Crown, most certainly had a family who loved him.

Father, what can I do? she beseeched, her inner prayer quickly interrupted by the man's agonized moan.

"D-don't leave me, missus . . . please s-stay. I don't want to . . . p-pass alone."

"I'm right here, John. I won't leave your side."

"Th-thank you, Missus Chilton."

"Deborah," she offered impulsively, squeezing his hand.

"Deborah," he repeated faintly. "I'm sorry—"

"Shhh, now. There's no need for apology."

"Jenny . . . my girl. White Plains. Letters in . . . my pocket . . . letters. One for Jenny . . . one for Ma."

"I'll see that your mail is delivered." Gently, Deborah removed the pair of envelopes from his breast pocket, flinching inwardly at the red-stained paper. Which would bring his dear ones most comfort? Which the greatest pain? John Kilby's words copied by the hand of another, or the loving words of his own hand, marked in his death-blood?

Setting the envelopes aside, she seated herself beside him, allowing her shoulder to rest against his.

A sigh left him and he leaned heavily upon her. "Do you believe . . . God is real?" he asked.

"I do," she affirmed, putting her arm all the way

around his shoulders. "Just as I believe His divine Son became man and died for our sins."

"Jesus," he breathed. "I want . . . Jesus."

"Aye, and I daresay He is well pleased with your hope in His infinite goodness. For God the Father 'shall deliver the needy when he crieth. . . . He shall redeem their soul from deceit and violence: and precious shall their blood be in His sight.' Cast yourself upon His mercy, good John, and allow Him to bear your sufferings."

A prayer for this unknown man, yet a brother in the Lord, welled up from inside her, and she interceded boldly on his behalf. Then there was nothing more to say, and she simply held him until he died.

As Deborah trudged into the house for a sheet, she wept at the loss of this man's life and for all others that had been taken in defense of this land. More tears fell while she struggled to bind his body into the linen, and for many minutes she couldn't rein in her despair at the thought that her beloved Paul might already lie dead in a nameless field. Into what kind of a world was their child about to be born? While she sewed shut the cloth, John's words came back to her, reminding her of the next task.

"Promise me you'll find someone—tonight! Promise!"

She had given her word, yet she had spoken honestly about those who remained in this area. There was no able-bodied man she dared trust with such a critical undertaking. She glanced about the shadowy barn, unable to put from her mind the scheme that had come to her previously.

She was reliable, she judged, possessing at times what might be considered a small amount of courage and perhaps a little resourcefulness as well. She had a horse. She was familiar with the countryside; she knew the route of which John had spoken. True, she was a woman, and one not far from her travail, at that. Yet who would suspect her of carrying papers to a general of the Continental Army?

Perhaps no one.

She herself would have to carry the intelligence John Kilby had set out to deliver.

She would do it for the sake of her country. She would ride for her husband and brothers, for all the patriotic men of New York and her America . . . and not least, for the brave soldier who had died on the floor of her barn.

The remainder of the night was a blur of preparations for her journey. Most difficult was digging a shallow grave at one end of her kitchen garden, with only the thin light of the moon to guide her efforts, then coaxing Duchess, the mare, to drag the courier's shrouded body to what she hoped would be its temporary resting place. There was no time to do anything more in the barn than cover the bloody hay with fresh, and to hope no enemy eyes would happen upon the Chilton homestead while she was away.

Just after two o'clock in the morning, a potent storm blew in from the northwest, and Deborah gave thanks to God for the good, hard rain that surely would sluice away tracks, trails, and revealing red traces. By four-thirty the downpour had abated to a cold drizzle, and she saddled Duchess. After giving the cows a portion of grain, she turned them into the paddock behind the barn and provided them with enough hay for several days. Deborah hoped they would still have a little milk when she returned from her journey, for cheese making was one of her livelihoods.

She had removed the documents from their leather pouch, which was now buried with its owner, and hastily sewn a drawstring pocket in which to carry them concealed from sight. The foreign presence beneath her clothing was disguised by her pregnancy, yet she was acutely aware of the small bundle pressing against the side of her abdomen. Her food and other necessities were tied in a roll behind her.

A cold mist was falling when Deborah departed. If by chance she could keep to the road and brazen her way south to Bemis Heights, it would be much faster than the cross-country route suggested by John Kilby. Weariness tugged at her eyelids as she considered what she might say if she was challenged. Surely it was feasible that a woman advanced in her pregnancy might want to visit her mother or sister.

The rain had turned the bumpy, furrowed track into muck, and Deborah was thankful for Duchess's strong legs and steady temperament. The next several hours passed without incident. By noon, patches of sunlight gleamed through hills covered with hardwood and fragrant pines. Birds twittered and squirrels scampered from tree to tree. If not for the pain and loneliness that dwelt inside her heavy heart, she might find it difficult to believe the country was at war.

Spying a glen beside a small creek, she guided Duchess to the spot. The grateful mare took a long drink while Deborah splashed water against her face. Then she opened her pack and ate a hasty repast of bread and cheese while Duchess grazed. Too soon, she forced herself to clamber back up into the saddle, not daring to rest without cover of darkness.

"Ho, ho, Cunningham! What haves we here?"

A pair of red-coated soldiers blocked her access back to the road. If John Kilby's information was accurate, this area could be thick with English. Oh, why hadn't she heeded the courier's advice to stay off the road? The tips of the British bayonets winked cruelly, giving her a visceral shiver.

"Your business?" the other, taller soldier inquired in a professional tone.

Duchess stepped in place nervously, and Deborah patted the mare's neck. "I just stopped for a bite."

"Aye, an' maybe I'll haves me a bite as well," the first man leered.

"You'll behave," the other said in a clipped

tone, shooting a quick glance of disapproval toward his partner. "Destination?" he went on, nodding toward Deborah.

She thought quickly. "Schenectady. To my mother's. My time draws close."

A volley of musket fire in the distance drew the men's attention for a few moments while Deborah frantically sorted through her meager options.

"Not today." The tone of the tall soldier was uncompromising, though his gaze was not unsympathetic. He leaned toward her and indicated that she fall in with them. "You'll be detained."

"You're arresting me? On what charge?"

"She coulds be a spy, Cunningham." The shorter man regarded her with sly eyes. "I says we search her right here."

Deborah struggled against the consuming impulse to lay her hand over the hidden documents. Like a brand, they burned white-hot against her flesh, for she knew the fate of spies was more often than not a swift execution. After hearing of the many atrocities perpetrated by the Redcoats, she had no reason to believe they'd hesitate to hang even a mother heavy with child.

"You'll be treated fairly until General Burgoyne has swept through." Again the tall man gestured for her to join them on the road.

They moved along at a brisk pace, evidently toward Burgoyne's camp. John Kilby had relayed that the Americans were well fortified at Bemis Heights. From the few fragments of conversation exchanged between these two soldiers, she gleaned that the enemy forces were amassing. She was obliged to ride ahead of them, precluding any possibility that she might lag behind or break away.

After they had covered some distance, the riders met up with a larger group of British soldiers. One of them wore the epaulette of an officer. While a brief parley ensued between the officer and the tall soldier who had detained her, the eyes of his oily colleague roved over her without cease. Did he truly suspect her of espionage, or were his motives simply licentious?

"You will go on with them." Speaking to her, the tall man interrupted her thoughts. "If you need to . . . refresh yourself, you may do so at this time."

He held Duchess's reins while Deborah dismounted, shrugging at her refusal of his assistance.

Inclining his head toward the woods, he bade her to make haste. She nodded her understanding, then walked laboriously into the thick cover of forest, exaggerating her infirmity as much as she dared, though truth be told, her legs and lower back ached fiercely. The babe stirred within her womb, its movement reassuring despite her present predicament.

Once she judged she was beyond the men's sight, she picked up her skirt and began to run. A mixture of fear and exultation gripped her, fueling her to greater speed. Later, if there was to be a later, she would grieve at having left Duchess in the hands of the British. She was certain, however, that her sturdy mount would have been confiscated no matter what.

Many times throughout the day Deborah had wondered what intelligence she carried. John Kilby, the dark-haired courier, had not disguised its importance. Could the documents she carried be so vital as to influence the outcome of the impending battle? the war?

She had to get through.

On she sped into the green darkness, lungs

burning and an agonizing stitch searing her side. Rocks and tree trunks wore beards of thick moss, while spindly ferns furled upward in their search for light. The ground was uneven, the terrain rough. More than once she stumbled, but terror kept her moving.

A shrill whistle sounded, followed by the far-away shouts of men. Her escape had been noticed. It would be nearly impossible to ride horseback in these woods, which added to her slim advantage. Even so, soldiers in prime condition could easily overtake a pregnant woman. Would her head start be enough?

Her spirit cried out for heavenly assistance as she pressed on. She came to a place where the trees thinned, their growth hampered by stone out-croppings. Perhaps if she kept to the stone for even a little distance, it might make her trail more diffi-cult to trace.

The whistle carried again, this time a little louder. *Merciful God, please save me!* The thought of be-ing captured by the crude, foul-mannered soldier spurred her to greater speed. As she risked a glance over her shoulder, the toe of her shoe caught in an uneven fissure, the interruption flinging her facedown against the unyielding surface. Her belly and the heels of her hands absorbed the greatest impact; nothing seemed to be broken. As she scrambled to her feet, she noticed that up ahead and to the right the ground sloped sharply downward. Without conscious thought, she ran to the ledge and climbed over it, searching for a cleft in the rock that might conceal her presence. Moving along the sharply slanted terrain was difficult, but finally she found what she was looking for: a long shelf with enough space beneath it to admit her body.

Unmindful of what creatures might inhabit the natural recess, she lay on her side and pushed herself to the back wall. The protuberance of her abdomen couldn't be helped, and she prayed she would not be noticed from above. Placing her hands over her mouth, she willed her breathing—which was coming in great, jagged gasps—to slow.

A few minutes later she heard the sound of her searchers.

"Fan out," came an angry, unfamiliar voice. "She can't have gotten far."

"My times are in Thy hand: deliver me from the hand of mine enemies," she silently pleaded in King David's words. *"Oh how great is Thy goodness, which Thou hast laid up for them that fear Thee; which Thou hast wrought for them that trust in Thee before the sons of men!"*

She moved one hand down from her face to cradle her belly, praying the baby hadn't been disturbed by her fall. Something scuttled across the back of her hand, and she squeezed her eyes shut tight to avoid crying out or moving.

"We haven't the time for this." She recognized the voice of the tall soldier, much nearer than the other voice had been.

"Capturing a spy is well worth our time," the unfamiliar man countered. The officer, she guessed. "Your partner seemed convinced she was suspicious."

"Wilkins's thoughts were of plunder, sir. He nurses a grudge because I refused him his way."

"Indeed? Nonetheless, we will continue the search. If the woman is found, she will be submitted to a thorough questioning."

Boots scuffed over the rocks for what seemed like an eternity more; then she heard nothing.

Were the men truly gone, or was the silence a ruse to draw her from her hiding place? She dared not move. Cramped and cold, she stayed beneath the outcropping until the indigo shadows of dusk surrendered their color to the night.

Slowly she emerged, clenching her jaw to keep from crying out as she forced her deadened limbs back into service. She was alone. Far above the strata of forest and thin-veiled clouds, a few stars gleamed soft white. The chill of the night kept the mosquitoes and punkies at bay, and for that small blessing amidst so many grave troubles, she was thankful.

The sky disappeared from view once she left the small clearing and reentered the thick woods. At the foot of a large tree, she curled up on the ground and tried to think of anything but the fact that not a soul on earth knew her whereabouts.

First emptiness, then despair, swept through her. Were a few pieces of paper worth all this? worth losing her life? She could destroy them, perhaps bury them, then return to the road in the morning. Even if she was captured and searched by the British, they would find no incriminating evidence. She would live.

Cramping hunger awakened her as the birds chirped in the dawn. Hardly believing she had slept, Deborah pushed herself to a sitting position, feeling pain in every part of her person. Her hands, knees, and elbows had been skinned in her fall. Lifting a hand to her face, she determined that her chin and left cheek had suffered similar damage.

Please, Father, she prayed, dissolving into dry, racking sobs. *There is no courage within me for this task. I'm so afraid . . . so tired. I fear all is lost. I am lost. Why does there have to be war? So much dying. Was there no other barn to which You could have sent John Kilby? You knew I would do this, didn't You? But now what do I do? Where do I go? I'm hungry. I'm cold. I am in pain.*

Even as she prayed, she knew she had no choice. Her country's future—and perhaps even her husband's life—depended on her completing this mission. She had given her word, and she had come so far. One life had been lost already because of the documents she carried. If she failed to deliver them, how many more men might die? Could she live the rest of her life with the horrible knowledge that she had chosen her own security over that of others?

A soft wind stirred the leaves above, the sound somehow calming her frenzied thoughts. God knew where she was, and He would be with her, no matter the outcome of the day. She stood, ignoring the pangs within her vitals. *Thank You for the gift of my life,* she adjoined, raising her hands to heaven. *Please help me to live the remainder of it as You would wish.*

Once the sun began its ascent, she determined her course and set off. At midday she came upon a creek, where she drank her fill, washed, and rested. When she arose she was light-headed, but she forced herself on, trying not to dwell on the fact that she was probably still in British-controlled territory.

At dusk, to anyone watching her progress, she would have appeared drunk. Her legs were wobbly, her steps staggering. The terrain had grown slanted, causing her calves to draw into excruciating knots. Beneath her breath, she sang psalms and hymns, sometimes not even realizing she was doing so. Many times she wondered if she were losing her mind.

By nightfall, she curled up beneath a large fir, its fallen needles a finer mattress than the one the forest had provided the night before. The babe was quiet, perhaps feeling the strain of physical hardship along with her. She fell into a void of dreamless sleep, arms cradled over her abdomen.

Deborah was awakened once again by the birds, and by the awareness of her physical misery. Her pelvis ached terribly as she moved. Sensations of hunger, nausea, intestinal cramping compounded the pain. All she'd had for food yesterday were a few handfuls of an unknown berry, which she'd cautiously tasted and found pleasant.

Her joints and muscles protested as she worked herself to her feet. As she began to walk, a feeling of unreality swept over her. Was it true that not even three days past, a Patriot courier had died in her barn . . . in her arms? Could she really be crossing British territory to deliver secret papers to a general of the Continental Army?

Filthy, starving, and sore, Deborah walked unsteadily throughout the day, resting often. She thought of Paul, and she bade him farewell in her heart as she prepared for what she believed was inevitable: She was going to die. Their precious, long-awaited baby was going to die. Praying for

God to prepare her for what was to come, she beseeched Him to forgive her sins and failings.

When the sun had passed its zenith, her senses were jolted by the sound of men talking and the flash of bright red uniforms. Heart pounding, she hugged the rough brown trunk of an oak tree and tried to make herself invisible. Long after they passed and their voices faded from hearing, she remained paralyzed. Go on? Why? Collapse or capture were her only two choices.

Finally, as the shadows grew longer, Deborah began to move in response to a nameless urgency that had come over her. She *had* to get to Bemis Heights or die trying. She could not spend one more night in the woods. Before long she came to a creek, stopping partway across it to gulp handfuls of cool, clear water.

"Halt!" a low voice commanded from the other side, nearly causing her knees to give way. A musket barrel emerged from the brush, followed by one man, then another. They wore not the hated red coats but homespun hunting jackets of drab brown. Taking her by the wrists, they pulled her into their hiding place in the brush along the bank.

"Who are you? Do you have any idea where you are, woman?" the man to her left growled. His lean face was tense, with more than a day's worth of whiskers adding to the roughness of his exterior.

Drained beyond all telling, Deborah shook her head.

"You cannot be here." The other man spoke up in a kindly tone. "This land is about to become a battleground."

"Are you Loyalist?" she whispered, looking into the face of the second man.

"Why do you ask?" His eyes widened, then narrowed.

The other man bit off a curse and released an infuriated sigh as he dropped her wrist.

"You are . . . American?" she asked, breathless, looking from the second man to the first.

The weight of their stares bored into her. Then the first man wheeled about and started to leave. The second man released her arm and turned to join him.

"No . . . wait," she implored. "I am American."

"Be whatever you like," the first man muttered. "We're leaving."

"I have dispatches for General Gates," she risked, knowing she did not have the strength to go much farther. She sank to her knees.

Both men stopped.

"John Kilby . . . a courier . . . was shot. He made me promise the intelligence he carried would reach the general at Bemis Heights."

"Where is Kilby now?" the first man asked, his voice sharp with suspicion.

"I buried him three nights past." Wrapping her arms around the curve of her abdomen, she repeated the password phrase Kilby had taught her, then slumped forward.

"Lieutenant Dean of the Continental Army at your service, Missus . . . ?" The first man's voice penetrated her consciousness as he helped her to her feet.

"Chilton . . . Deborah. My husband is—"

"Good heavens . . . our captain!" he completed before addressing the other man. "Soldier, we will be escorting Missus Chilton to camp posthaste."

"Yes, Lieutenant," the second replied, lifting Deborah into his arms as if she weighed no more than a few sticks of kindling.

For a moment she struggled, before allowing her head to rest against his chest. "How far?" she asked in weary apology.

"It will be an honor to carry you the three miles to camp, Mrs. Chilton," the soldier replied formally, his deep brown eyes regarding her with a mixture of awe and compassion.

Lieutenant Dean addressed Deborah again. "You have done our army and our countrymen invaluable service—obviously at great personal sacrifice. We are in your debt."

At the word *sacrifice,* hot tears rushed to her eyes. The price of freedom was so dear. Beneath her hands was the packet of messages for which John Kilby had died. For that, a mother would grieve her lost son; a young woman would mourn the handsome suitor who would never return to become her husband.

And another sacrifice had been made this day as well. As Deborah cupped the roundness of her belly, she was no longer able to ignore what she did not want to face. Her womb was silent, and it had been so since her fall upon the rock. What would she say to Paul? A sob caught in her throat, and she buried her face in the soldier's coat and wept.

As she dressed for her son's graduation ceremony, Meg reflected on Deborah Chilton's incredible bravery in carrying John Kilby's dispatches to General Gates in 1777. Again and again in the past days, she had called up images of that brave young woman's flight across enemy-controlled territory. While Meg was unwilling to allow Tyler to enlist in the Army, Deborah had risked the life of a child— her firstborn child—in her attempt to ensure the freedom of her country. No, Meg clarified, Deborah hadn't just risked her baby's life—she had sacrificed it.

Had Deborah's efforts been worth such a terrible loss? Meg cringed inwardly at the words that had flown so readily from her tongue the afternoon of Tyler's announcement. "You're my only son, and I will never give you my blessing," she had told him. Deborah had had nothing more than the promise of a long-anticipated child, but for the sake of her country, she willingly surrendered her right to give birth, to enjoy watching her baby grow into a healthy adult, to experience the lifetime of satisfaction that motherhood could bring.

A stubborn zipper brought Meg back to the present. "Dan, will you help me with this?"

Her husband had been staring at his three good ties for at least ten minutes, clearly undecided on the right one for such an occasion. Looking almost relieved to set aside the task, he stepped to Meg's side and went to work on the zipper.

"I guess I just assumed Tyler wanted to study computer science, didn't you?" she asked as he fastened the hook on the navy silk dress she had chosen for this special day. "That's what he's been telling us for years."

"I know. Since seventh grade." Dan grabbed a tie and began crafting a four-in-hand knot, a rarity for a man who spent his days loading boxes in a cosmetics factory. He frowned, glancing back and forth between the mirror and his neckwear. A man of few words, he nonetheless loved his wife and son with a passion that was obvious to everyone.

"Where do you suppose he got this harebrained idea to enlist in the Army?" Meg asked. "Do you think a recruiter went to the high school and talked him into it?"

"They probably had an assembly or something." He was silent a moment. "You know, it's one thing to listen to a recruiter. But it's something else again to decide to enlist. That takes courage."

Again, Deborah Chilton's bravery slipped into Meg's thoughts. She remembered thinking that no woman of good conscience would willingly risk the life of her only child. *It is a woman's duty to love and protect her offspring,* she told herself, *and no military or political cause could possibly be great enough to lead her to willingly sacrifice that loved one.* Did Deborah Chilton's willing sacrifice make her a bad woman? What did it say about all the mothers who had watched their only sons go off to war throughout the centuries? Had they been wrong?

Or were they heroines of history?

The more she thought about it, the more Meg knew that Tyler's argument about the "spare child" had merit. The fact that he was an only child was not a valid enough reason to oppose his decision. All the same, she wasn't ready to back down and grant her permission. And she wasn't about to pronounce her blessing on it.

"Well, I don't see how he could even think of giving up that scholarship to Yale," she told her husband. "It doesn't make sense to me."

"Me neither."

Why in the world wouldn't Tyler do the reasonable thing and go to college like he'd planned? To Meg, that incredible opportunity was a clear gift from God—an obvious sign of His will for Tyler's future. And it far outweighed her son's "feeling" that he ought to enlist in the Army.

Meg had been through too much in her life to count on emotion or intuition as a sign of God's hand. She relied on concrete evidence. At eighteen, she had watched the man she loved go off to fight in the jungles of Southeast Asia. She had prayed for Dan's safety during those long months, but he had returned to her ravaged by disease and irrevocably scarred from his experience. Meg's faith in God had faltered at first. In time, she saw the evidence of God's presence. After all, he had spared Dan's life and allowed them to marry.

The same thing occurred when they had been unable to conceive a child, because Dan's malarial fever had all but sterilized him. Meg's response

had alternated between despair and stoic accep-
tance. Then her completely unexpected pregnancy
told her that God did want her to have a child. A
son. A beautiful baby boy—a touchable, huggable
reminder that God spoke in realities, not emo-
tions.

"Well, have you talked to your son about this situation?" Meg asked Dan.

"Haven't seen hide nor hair of him lately."

"You don't think he ought to do it, do you?
Join the Army, I mean? Give up his scholarship?"

"It's a big decision."

"Yes, I know, but what do you think, honey? I
think we ought to just flat-out tell him no. I mean,
we are his parents. We should still have some influence over him, even though he's eighteen, shouldn't
we? We raised him, and we know what's best for him.
And we have the perspective of experience. You went
to Vietnam. You wouldn't want your son to go
through something like you did, would you?"

"No." He tugged on his tie, realizing with a
frown that the narrower tail was too long. "Rats! I
hate these things."

"Just make a regular knot, Dan."

"Not for Tyler's graduation. I gotta have the real thing." He started over.

The strained atmosphere in the house these past few days was almost more than Meg could bear. Dan was reluctant to talk about Tyler's decision to join the Army, and his silence grated like steel against rock. The few times Meg had tried to bring up the subject with her son had ended with her blowing up in anger or dissolving in tears. So Tyler had made himself scarce—using the excuse that he wouldn't be able to spend much time with his friends after graduation. His mother knew better.

Tyler was a great kid, the best any parent could hope for, Meg thought as she worked her feet into navy leather pumps. His Christian faith shined through his behavior and the choices he made. His intelligence allowed him to grasp anything on which he focused it. Sure, he was all boy—with the smelly track shoes, belching contests, and sometimes sloppy manners that went along with it. But all in all, Meg couldn't be prouder of him, and she had long cherished great expectations for his future.

"Did Jake call this morning?" Dan asked as he reworked his tie. "He and Martha were supposed to get in late last night, and he said he'd call here to get directions to the high school."

"I haven't heard from him." Meg fastened a string of her mother's pearls around her throat. "I don't want him to do it," she said, unable to drop the subject. "I don't want him to enlist. Most kids do this kind of thing to pay for college. Tyler doesn't need that. I just can't figure it out."

"He says God told him to join the Army." Dan straightened his tie, perfect at last. "I don't think we can argue against that, Meg."

"I can argue with it. I can argue plenty. It's clear to me that his scholarship to Yale is a God-given blessing. It's ordained. Every road sign points to it. And there's nothing—not one single thing—that could possibly point to the military."

"Except what's in Tyler's heart."

Meg looked at her husband. He was a good man, a hard worker, a devoted husband and father. A churchgoer. And Dan was intelligent—he could fix anything, and he read voraciously. Meg knew Tyler got most of his brains from his father.

Not that she wasn't smart. She had a college degree, and her career as a designer for a linens company was becoming more profitable each year. But she had always wanted more for Tyler. He was capable of so much! A career creating software, a company of his own, a large house, a lovely wife and children. Oh, he could have anything he wanted—but not if he joined the military and got himself shot down in a desert in some foreign country whose name ended with -*stan*.

"Well, I wouldn't trust what's in the heart of an eighteen-year-old boy," she objected. "What can he possibly know about life?"

"When I was eighteen, you were in my heart, Meg. That was all I needed to know about life. And it was the right thing."

She mustered a smile. "I know, honey. We were in love. But I just don't think Tyler is able to discern the long-term ramifications of this decision. The Army could completely destroy him—physically, mentally, emotionally, spiritually."

"Or it could build him into exactly the man God wants him to be."

"Are you agreeing with Tyler?" she demanded, turning on her husband. "Do you actually think he should do this?"

Dan shrugged. "I think we'd better start calling hotels, is what I think. If Jake and Martha aren't in town yet, things are going to be a mess. You know how my brother is about directions. He might come all this way to see his nephew graduate and then miss the whole shebang."

"They were going to stay at the Ramada. I'll call and see if they're in yet." Meg started for the door, but her husband's voice stopped her.

"Meg, honey, try not to fret so much," Dan said gently. "Tyler was never ours to begin with, you know. We only have him because God chose to give him to us. He's belonged to God from before he was ever born. We have to let him go now."

Meg stared at her husband's handsome face, his blue eyes soft and warm. "I don't want him to die," she whispered. "Not so young. I don't want him to get hurt in any way. Oh, Dan, I'm scared. I'm afraid we'll lose our son."

He wrapped his arms around her and held her close. "Let's don't think about that, sweetheart. Let's enjoy this special day. You got that genealogy chart ready? He's gonna love it."

"I changed my mind about giving it to him."

He drew back and looked down into her eyes. "How come? I thought you had it all ready. Especially after I found that box in my mother's attic."

She shook her head. "It's that Deborah Chilton. I don't want Tyler to read about her."

"She did something bad? I thought you said she was a hero."

"Well, she was—but look what it cost her. She lost her child. Her precious baby! I mean, is that what it takes? Is that what God wants? Am I supposed to sacrifice my only son?"

Even as she spoke the words, she realized again how selfish they sounded. Her eyes filling with tears for the hundredth time since Tyler's announcement, Meg pulled out of her husband's arms. "I'd better go call the hotel."

Pressing back the hurt and fear, Meg hurried to the phone. In moments, she was speaking with her sister-in-law. Martha and Jake had arrived safely in the middle of the night, and they had slept in. Martha assured her they were already dressed and would be at the high school on time.

"Tyler!" Dan called as he headed for the front door. "You coming with us?"

"I'll take my car."

"Oh, come with us," Meg pleaded. "Then we can all ride to dinner together."

"Okay, sure."

Tyler stepped out of his bedroom, and Meg's knees nearly buckled. How handsome he was. How grown-up in his black suit and tie. Oh, dear heaven, he was an adult.

"You look wonderful," she managed. "Wow. I'm so proud of you, honey."

"Thanks, Mom." He grinned, shy dimples carving into his cheeks. "Do you think the tie tack is too much? It was Grandpa Irving's."

"It's perfect. Dad is going to be so touched that you're wearing it."

"Can you help me with my cap? It keeps sliding off."

"I'll get some bobby pins!"

"Bobby pins? No way!"

"Yes, way. Everybody's going to have their caps bobby-pinned on. Just a sec." She rounded up a handful of pins and hurried out the door after her husband and son.

Before long they were joining the crowd of parents and siblings, grandparents and cousins, aunts and uncles walking toward the high school gym.

"There they are!" Tyler called out, pointing across the crowd at a couple standing alone under a tree. "Hey, Uncle Jake! Aunt Martha!"

"Tyler!" Jake waved and took his wife's hand as they started across the commons to greet their nephew. "You're so tall these days! Why, I believe you've grown two inches since we last saw you, boy!"

"And handsome!" Martha beamed, as proud as if Tyler were their own son. Childless, the couple had poured their love and attention on him, and Meg knew Tyler adored them.

"Thanks for driving all this way, Uncle Jake," Tyler said.

"Wouldn't have missed it for the world."

"Now, when do you leave for Yale?" Martha said as the small group started for the gym again. "Ooo, just saying 'Yale' makes me shiver. I never thought I'd see the day when one of our own went to an Ivy League university!"

"I guess Mom didn't tell you there's been a change, Aunt Martha," Tyler replied, his long stride forcing everyone to scramble to keep up. "I decided to join the Army instead. I'm planning to enlist next week."

"The Army?" Martha glanced at Meg. "That *is* a big change. You never mentioned this."

"No," Meg said. "And I don't think he should do it. In fact, I'm totally opposed to the idea. It's not every young man who can earn a full scholarship to a school like Yale."

"So you think I'm too smart to join the military, Mom?" Tyler asked.

"As a matter of fact, I do. God gave you an incredible intelligence, and you have an obligation to develop it to the highest level. At Yale."

"So you're saying the brightest of America's youth ought to go to college and then into business. You don't think the armed services need us, do you? You don't think we ought to be asked to defend our fellow citizens because we're too smart."

"Tyler, please."

He stopped and faced her as the throng swept around them on either side. "What are you thinking, Mom?" he challenged in a low voice. "Only

Joe Average ought to protect our country? Keep the smart ones at home, send the slower boys out there to get killed. Is that what you advocate?"

"No, Tyler."

"Yes, that is what you think. And it's wrong, Mom. So wrong. They need me, and I want to serve."

"Why?"

"Because I can. Because I'm good enough. Because it's what God wants of me."

"Hey, you two," Dan said, working his way back toward them. "You're holding things up. Come on inside, and let's leave this till later."

"Give me your blessing, Mom," Tyler implored, his blue eyes never wavering from his mother's face. "Please."

She looked away, her throat tight. "No, Tyler. The truth is, you *are* too smart. You're too smart to trade a wonderful education and a brilliant career for years of uncertainty and danger. And yes, you are too smart to waste your God-given brains out on some battlefield. It doesn't take your kind of intelligence to do what's required of the average soldier, and I won't bless a wrong decision. I won't."

With a harsh sigh, he swung around on his heel. "I'll meet you at the car after the ceremony, Dad."

Meg scrounged in her pocket for a tissue as Dan slipped an arm around her shoulders. When they rejoined the others, Jake patted her hand.

"It's rough, huh? They get to be eighteen, and they make up their own mind about things. You can't hardly stop 'em, Meg."

"I agree with Meg," Martha said as they found places on the bleachers. "Tyler is so smart—just look at that GPA! I think he ought to go on to Yale. An opportunity like this comes once in a lifetime, if at all. Besides, I wouldn't want him off in a foreign country, would you, Jake? Risking his life . . . maybe getting shot or blown up?"

"No, I wouldn't." Jake straightened suddenly. "Hey, that reminds me, Meg. I was going through some of Mom's old papers the other day, and I came across this envelope. I thought you'd want to take a look at what's in it, seeing as how you're collecting stuff to put on Tyler's genealogy chart."

"She's changed her mind about giving it to him," Dan said, leaning across Meg.

"Oh, just let me see what you found, Jake." Meg took the manila envelope and drew out a small medal awarded for valor. As the strains of "Pomp and Circumstance" filtered up from the band pit, she slid out a framed letter on which a silver cross had been mounted.

"The Maxwell Cross!" she cried out, jerking upright. "Elizabeth Chilton was awarded the Maxwell Cross. And the letter of commendation is actually signed by Major General Maxwell!"

"Yep, but it ain't worth much. Maxwell signed all kinds of papers over his lifetime. Oh, it's a nice collector's item, but I thought it would mean more to you for your genealogy work."

Again, Meg sank into herself, thinking of the woman whose portrait graced the pale blue mat and silver frame on her desk. Meg didn't know much about Elizabeth Rogers Chilton, except that she had been an ordinary woman who had lived during a difficult period in the history of the United States. While the country was ripped apart by civil war, the young, unmarried Elizabeth Rogers had served as a nurse. Later, she married Alden

Eugene Chilton and gave birth to six children, two of whom died before adulthood. Clearly, Elizabeth had experienced hardship, but nothing out of the ordinary. She was just a common, undistinguished woman, Meg had always believed.

Now, holding the medal and letter of commendation, Meg thought of her own rationale that Tyler was too smart to serve as a soldier. Extraordinary intelligence was needed more for civilian than military duty, wasn't it? That was how a country grew.

Certain she was right, Meg bent her head to scan the letter that accompanied Elizabeth Chilton's Maxwell Cross. As the graduates filed into the gymnasium, she absorbed the words written in a flowing hand:

I, Major General John Maxwell of the Union Army, do hereby commend Miss Elizabeth Rogers for her valor upon the battlefield at Chancellorsville, Virginia. Miss Rogers, a volunteer nurse with the Third Michigan, did selflessly and without heed for her own safety . . .

Chancellorsville, Virginia
May 1863

In this midnight engagement, the wounded and dead fell more rapidly than flies descending upon a morbid feast. Exploding artillery and howling cannonballs snuffed lives and severed limbs, while whizzing minié balls—.56 caliber slugs—wrought their own brand of destruction. Indistinguishable screams, curses, groans, and shouts added to the clamoring inferno of sight and sound.

Elizabeth Rogers, a volunteer nurse with the Third Michigan Infantry, had grown accustomed to the hellish din of combat. She had served in the battle of Blackburn's Ford, both battles at Bull Run, Antietam, and Fredericksburg. Now, at Chancellorsville, she continued to do what she could for the fallen soldiers, whether it be dressing their wounds, claiming them from the battlefield, or whispering kind words to those who would not survive the night. She washed faces, wiped brows, and tended unimaginable horrors. Not the least of those were the deadly diseases that often plagued the camps. All too frequently she closed the lids of eyes that would see no more.

As Elizabeth urged her horse forward, trailing in Major General Sickles's late-night advance, she prayed for heavenly guidance as well as for the shrewdness to save as many men as she could. It remained a mystery to her how she had escaped death as many times as she had. Her last mount, a gelding, had been shot out from under her. She added a brief prayer of protection for her fine-tempered mare throughout this new campaign.

Elizabeth's widowed father had thought her mad when she resigned her clerical position at the start of the war to volunteer, initially, as a laundress. "Oh, Lizzie, what have you done?" he cried, sadness and disappointment mingling in his gaze. "You've a stable and respectable position, not to mention a mind for facts and numbers that could set a university professor on his ear. Why would you squander such blessings in order to do something so tedious as to boil soldiers' dirty clothing? You're too intelligent for such well-meaning but ill-placed sentiment."

Indeed, there were still moments when she agreed wholeheartedly with Father's assessment. Long gone were most of the females who had volunteered for service in this regiment at the war's outset, having returned to the safety of their Northern homes. As the war intensified and casualties increased, the few of them that remained had been shifted from doing laundry to providing nursing care for the wounded. Father was no more pleased by this than he was with her initial duties, but something amidst the ghastly, gruesome scenes she witnessed compelled Elizabeth to continue giving what she could. Compared to the sacrifices of the soldiers, the forfeit of herself was a humble offering indeed.

She knew she was not a comely woman. She did not possess fine-boned features, spun-gold curls, or long-lashed eyes that mirrored the summer sky. Rather, Providence had seen fit to equip her with broad shoulders, a strong back, and serious brown eyes set into an unremarkable face. Fancy feminine trappings looked as out of place on her as earrings on a draft horse. Yet she had the respect and appreciation of the men she tended, and had long since stopped counting the number of impulsive marriage proposals she had received.

Elizabeth did not consider herself particularly courageous, but she was not afraid to die. Her arm had once been grazed by a bullet, and the black skirt she wore this night carried a pair of patches—one in front and one in back—where a minié ball had passed between her knees. Rather than bearing a fatalistic attitude about her vocation, she prayed that she might recognize each soul before her as a brother sojourner of this world fashioned by the almighty Father Himself. Each day she prayed that her thoughts, words, and deeds might bear witness to the words and example of God the Son.

If, in the course of her labors, her life should be asked for, then so be it.

"Water," came the piteous call that she heard countless times each day. The wounded, especially those with mortal wounds to the belly, were the thirstiest. Their pleas were heartrending, their deaths often lingering. She dismounted her horse as she spotted a lad on the ground, horribly injured, his age not more than seventeen. After wetting a cloth and dampening his lips, she touched his pale forehead and prayed for God's mercy to be upon him.

"Thank you," he choked out, trying to smile. "I think you must be an angel."

Moving this poor boy was impossible at the moment. Fighting continued on all sides. A nearly full moon lit the occasional clearing, but in the forest the darkness was almost complete. Bright flashes of musket fire and artillery revealed positions, but whose? Elizabeth mounted her mare and traveled on, straining to catch sight of fallen Union soldiers.

General "Fighting Joe" Hooker's brash assurances that he would trounce Lee's army were not materializing. In fact, before dark the Eleventh Corps had been crushed by Stonewall Jackson's sudden, breathtaking assault. The Federals had forfeited two miles of ground. Several Union officers had condemned Hooker's failure to press forward while he'd had the advantage.

The brigade with which Elizabeth rode this night had been moving through a thickly forested area when it ran headlong into advancing Confederate troops. Pandemonium reigned as many Union soldiers became separated from their regiments. Worse, many troops fired upon their own. Not a few men retreated in terror. Their officers shouted, urging them to do their duty, to hold fast. Some did just that, checking their retreat and turning back. Elizabeth witnessed others being convinced at bayonet point.

How many soldiers she assisted in the next hour was impossible to say. At some point she became separated from the surgeon's aide, who routinely followed her and bore the medicine chest. Her canteen had grown light, and her saddlebag was emptying of its lint and bandages at a rapid rate. She was bent over a gruesome leg wound when a voice came from over her shoulder.

"Miss Elizabeth Rogers, you are to fall back without delay."

A double row of brass buttons winked from the officer's breast. The hooves of the large, dark horse upon which he sat were impatient, wanting to move. A cannonade howled then, briefly illuminating the area, revealing men in various postures. Curses, screams, and cheers rose up. Riderless horses bolted wildly.

"Colonel, I can't," she pleaded. "There are—"

"Without delay," he repeated sternly. "It is too hot here."

She acquiesced, nodding. "Yes, sir. Once this bandage is on."

He nodded, kicked his horse, and rode off. After murmuring encouragement to the semiconscious man, Elizabeth took to her saddle. She passed through a long stretch of woods before becoming enveloped in a boggy area, its rising mists mingling with the acrid gun smoke that thickened the air. Though the battle raged not far away, this little clearing seemed eerily quiet.

A moment of indecision stopped her. She had thought she was heading toward the rear, but maybe she had gotten turned around. She brought her mare about, prepared to cautiously retrace her course, when she heard a faint cry.

"Please . . . help me."

Reversing, she headed toward the source of the sound—a nearby stand of trees. She reached into the saddlebag for a roll of bandage. At the woods' edge she dismounted, the marshy ground sucking at her feet.

From ahead and to the right came the hoarse whisper. "Thank God you have come. My aide is dead."

Elizabeth stumbled over a limp form and barely kept her balance. A few feet ahead was the dark outline of a man beside a tree. An arm came up slowly and he groaned in pain.

"Are you Miss Elizabeth of Michigan?"

"I am. But I do not recognize your voice, sir."

"Major General Maxwell," he grunted while Elizabeth knelt, astonished at her patient's identity. A major general, here? "Woke up . . . moonlight . . . could see you sitting sidesaddle. Thought I was dreaming . . ."

"Shhh, sir. How did you come to be here? Where are you wounded?"

"Think . . . ball in my shoulder. Can't move the arm. Rebels took this ground."

His deduction about the damage was correct. The slickness of blood greeted her assessing fingers, and she quickly packed the wound, stanching its flow. In the faint moonlight penetrating the screen of the trees, she noticed a sizeable laceration upon her patient's brow. It too had bled a great deal. With the remaining water in her canteen, she washed the gash and gave the general a few sips to drink.

"Time to move you to the rear. I'll get my horse." She had walked only a few steps when she heard musket fire and bloodcurdling whoops of Rebel jubilation. The normally steadfast mare reared and bolted; quickly Elizabeth returned to Maxwell, who was shivering.

". . . some Yankee dogs over this way," one voice carried across the marshy area. "Wolsely thinks he winged an officer."

Elizabeth swallowed hard. "I can't move you," she whispered, her mind seizing upon a wild ploy. "But God willing, I can protect you from capture."

Before he could reply, she hastened to the body of his aide and deftly stripped off the dead man's uniform. His shirt was soaked with blood, for the unfortunate fellow had been shot in the chest. Heedless of that, Elizabeth donned the jacket. Then after removing her skirt and petticoats, she put on his trousers. They were too big, but they would stay in place, she judged. After ripping off the identifying corps badge, she jammed the man's hat onto her head, realizing there was nothing to do about her hair but cover it. She ran back to Maxwell and disguised him with her clothing, taking care to keep the lighter, more visible color of her petticoats pushed beneath the dark skirt. Finally, she added what loose brush was within reach.

"You must not make a sound," she instructed. "Not until our boys take back this ground. Do not doubt they will, General. Be assured I will be praying this happens soon."

"You cannot—"

Elizabeth silenced him with her finger over his lips. "Not a sound. I must go."

If she could skirt the clearing and take a position on the other side, she might be able to keep the Rebel troops from discovering Maxwell. She prayed for the general's safety as she dashed along the tree line. Musket shots and flashes of light grew closer from between the trees.

Finally she dared go no farther for fear of being cut down. She dove to the ground and took shelter at the foot of a large tree. It was not difficult to imitate the sounds of agony that rang across killing fields and filled hospital wards.

"Wounded!" she cried amidst her groans and moaning. "I surrender!"

Her captors were a pair of brusque North Carolinians, who hauled her to her feet and began marching her to the Confederate rear. They cared not who their prisoner was—only that he could manage walking. Elizabeth kept her head down and one hand over the front of her borrowed, bloodstained coat. After a long march they reached a place where several prisoners were gathered. A few lamps hung from poles, and two large pots of coffee steamed over a fire. The two men left her and poured themselves coffee, while she waited for what seemed a very long time to be questioned.

The mood of the Union prisoners was subdued. Many bore wounds, and Elizabeth knelt beside the nearest, a corporal. She learned his forearm had been broken when he'd tumbled from his horse after it was cut down by a Confederate bullet.

"I need a splint," she called. One of the soldiers produced a stick.

"You know something about doctoring?" The corporal's voice was tight with pain.

She nodded as she fastened the splint with strips of a uniform sleeve donated by a nearby private.

"What's your regiment?" the corporal asked, squinting at her hat. "Your badge is gone."

Another voice interrupted. "Hey, you need to take a look at Packard's leg. It won't stop bleeding."

She shrugged at the corporal before rising and moving on to a man who held his leg in mute anguish. It was a terrible frustration not to have her saddlebag with her.

Though supported by his friends, Packard, a husky lad of twenty, was still on his feet, an encouraging sign.

"You're not taking my leg!" the young man vowed, warning her away with an expression of desperation. Though someone had lashed a blanket to his thigh with a belt, blood had soaked through the makeshift dressing. He cursed roundly before adding, "The devil take you if you think you're going to saw me in two!"

"I only want a look," she replied evenly, holding up her hands to show that she carried neither bone saws nor surgical knives. Glancing about, she asked, "Does anyone have a clean cloth?"

Kneeling before the man, she gently exposed the injury. Though the skin and thigh muscles above his knee had been torn quite cruelly, the bullet had missed the bone. Packard was one of the lucky ones. As long as gangrene or erysipelas did not set in, he would keep his leg.

A shirt of dubious cleanliness was placed in her hand, and she pressed it firmly against the ragged flesh. Rather than relying on the belt to stanch the flow of blood, she bade one of the nearby soldiers to apply direct pressure to the area.

"Thank you," Packard ground out, having suffered her ministrations without making a sound. As she stood, his gaze went to her torso. "Looks like you took one too."

"Not my blood," she replied truthfully, her arm already being tugged at by another man wanting attention for his comrade.

Beyond being captured, Elizabeth had not stopped to think through the possible consequences of impersonating Maxwell's aide. What was she to do? Dare she expose her identity, or was it

best to keep silent and play her new role to its con-
clusion? What if someone were to recognize her?

In her course of service to the Union Army, she
had discovered half a dozen women clad as male
soldiers, four among the dead and two wounded.
She had also heard of this phenomenon amongst
the Confederates. Though she could well conceive
of the patriotism that inspired the gentler sex to go
to such lengths to fight for their ideals, she also realized that to some, the presence of women in battle was a grievous offense.

But before she could dwell on this any further,
another patient was before her. The soldier's face
and hands had been burned black by exploding artillery. Miraculously, the rest of him seemed to be
unharmed. As she began her work, praying that the
enemy guards might grant her the clean water and
dressings she had sent a Union officer to ask for,
her thoughts turned to Maxwell. Had the Federals
taken back the ground upon which he lay? Or did
he yet languish between the lines? Dare she hope
that he had been rescued? And if so, had he been
discovered by his own men or by the Confederates?
A captured major general would be a prize, indeed.

"Surgeon? We need a surgeon!" A determined man pushed through the crowd, jostling those near her. One man lost his balance, and his flailing arm knocked the hat from her head.

"Good night!" someone exclaimed. "Look at his hair!"

"*His* hair! That ain't no man, Wilder, 'less I don't know absolutely nothin' about nothin'!"

"There's a woman here?" a deep-pitched voice inquired.

A ripple of shock spread through those assembled nearby, producing apprehension on some faces and grins on others.

"Who are you?" the burned man whispered.

"I know who she is!" yet another voice supplied. "That's Miss Elizabeth, the angel of the battlefield. You don't know me, but I saw you at Antietam Creek, ma'am. Fifth Michigan?"

"Third," she softly corrected.

"What happened to you?" the same man asked. "Were you shot? Where are your skirts?"

"I am unharmed. The uniform is . . . on loan."

"Now *here's* a story for my grandchildren," another man quipped. "If I live to have any."

"Quiet down, everyone. Put this back on," directed the man who had identified her. He handed Elizabeth the hat. "We can't have the Johnnies knowing they've captured a woman."

"But what are we going to do with her?" came a nervous query from someone in the crowd.

"Don't worry, Miss Elizabeth; we'll keep you safe," the man with the deep-pitched voice promised. Others echoed his sentiment.

This assurance from weaponless prisoners of war touched her. But before she could form a reply, a ruddy-cheeked guard pushed his way toward her.

"Where's the woman?" he demanded to know.

"Woman? What woman?" A babble of voices rose to distract him. "The night air must be playin' tricks on your mind. There's no woman here."

"I got ears, an' I heard you say a woman was here. Now where is she? Or do I have to start strippin' you all, one by one?"

"I am here," Elizabeth spoke up.

The guard's eyes widened as he studied her face. "Come with me. My commander will be mighty interested in talking with you."

She hesitated. "Please . . . can you promise me this man's burns will be attended?"

"The wounded aren't my affair." He gestured with his rifle. "This way."

"Careful," a nearby Union officer warned. "If you don't treat her right, I'll make it my business to come looking for you."

"I don't know what regard you Yankees have for womenfolk," the guard retorted, "but we Southerners are *gentlemen.*"

"She's a nurse," pleaded a soldier who supported his bleeding, suffering friend. "She's *our* nurse! Look at all the wounded who aren't bad off enough for your hospital. We need Miss Elizabeth, mister, and we need some supplies. Can't you leave her with us?"

The guard was adamant. *"Miss Elizabeth* comes with me. The rest of you can wait your turn for attention, just like everyone else."

"Sir, I beg you for some clean bandages for this man," Elizabeth entreated. "If your position were reversed with that of his, wouldn't you want your burns to be covered?"

"I-I . . . ," he stammered, hesitating. He looked

briefly into Elizabeth's face, and then at the ground, mumbling, "I'll see what I can do." After clearing his throat, he added with more vigor, "Now, if you will please come with me."

"Thank you." Elizabeth was taken to a tent and told to wait while the guard had a conversation with an officer. This process was repeated, and finally she was admitted to a third officer's tent. Inside was a bearded, tired-looking man in his shirtsleeves. He sighed heavily and stood up when she entered, indicating a canvas chair opposite him.

"I am told you are a nurse for the Union Army," he began without preamble. "Yet you are dressed in the clothing of a soldier who, by my reckoning, has departed this life. Why, I wonder?"

"I thought it prudent, sir."

"Prudent? How so?" Flickering lamplight made dark shadows beneath his eyes more prominent. He sighed again, with all the appearance of a man gathering his last reserves, and toyed with the plume of the hat that sat on the table.

Throughout this long night, there had been no sleep for anyone but the dead. What the dawn would hold was impossible to predict, but Elizabeth suspected this day would be one of heavy engagement . . . and heavy casualties. Weary of body and spirit herself, she spoke plainly, seeing no reason to disguise the truth.

"I sought to protect the identity of another and so offered myself up for capture."

Eyebrows raised, the man studied her for a long moment before looking away toward the corner of the tent. "'Loyalty is still the same,'" he quoted faintly, "'whether it win or lose the game.'" After another silence, he spoke as if with some effort. "This night has seen sufficient tragedy. Don't you agree?"

Not certain what he was asking, she finally inquired, "Sir?"

He did not answer her, but stood and called for the guard. When the ruddy-cheeked sentinel opened the tent flap, the bearded officer pointed for her to accompany him. "Miss Elizabeth, nurse of the Union Army," he said as she started to leave, "is granted unconditional release. We do not take female prisoners. She will be escorted to the front, and from there will make her way on her own."

"Th-thank you," she stammered, hardly believing what had just transpired.

In no time she was mounted on a tall horse and led to the Confederate line by a pair of courteous sentries. From them she learned that their beloved General Jackson had been wounded only hours earlier. Was that what the bearded man had meant by the night's having seen enough tragedy?

After the sentries left her, Elizabeth faced the question of how to safely traverse the ground between the lines. Then a Union scout happened upon her and guided her back to camp. They passed lines of sturdy breastworks, constructed during the night by Union soldiers in preparation for the coming battle.

After she had eaten some hardtack and drunk two cups of coffee, she discarded the ragged, bloodstained uniform, washed in cold water, and changed into her only remaining skirt and blouse. Dawn was breaking when she entered the hospital tent, just as she had done so many other mornings.

Though she was rarely given to feeling morose, she looked about at the wounded and dying and wondered at her purpose amidst all this calamity. So many lives had been lost—on both sides. She'd volunteered for the Union Army with high ideals, first as a laundress, and not long afterward accepting the role of a nurse. Had the past two years of her life really amounted to anything? made any difference? Her fatigue fully consumed the exhausted joy she had felt at her release.

Father, she began her morning offering, the smells of sickness, elimination, and decaying flesh filling her nostrils. *Help me to serve You today as I—*

"Elizabeth!" gasped Bridget, a fellow nurse, interrupting her prayers. The woman's loud whisper carried through the tent. "How did you get back? Mercy! I heard about what you did!"

The normally laconic Dr. Jahnke looked up from his task of removing a ball from the hand of a chloroformed soldier. He granted her one of his rare, faint smiles. "There's someone who would like to speak with you, someone who's most grateful for the quick mind you possess."

"Over here," Bridget directed, taking her arm. "He's just had surgery."

The man on the cot was pale, his face stubbled

with a day's growth of whiskers. A white bandage swathed his forehead; another was wrapped around his shoulder. His eyes flickered at her approach, their lids heavy with the effects of sedation.

"Ahh . . ." he said thickly, trying to lick his lips. "You . . ."

"General Maxwell?" she whispered, overcome with emotion.

He winced in pain as he moved to offer her his good hand. "I . . . owe you—"

"Oh, no . . . you owe me nothing, sir," she interrupted, clasping both her hands around his one. "What we both owe is thanks to our God."

For a long moment he stared into her eyes. Then slowly his awareness faded as sleep overcame him. He did not stir when, a moment later, the first sounds of artillery fire rent the air, followed by the report of thousands of rifles.

Automatically, Elizabeth stepped outside, wiping the dampness from her cheeks. Tempting as it was to pause for reflection on all that had occurred during the night, her duty lay out there, among the men who lived and bled and died on the lines. "I need a fresh horse!" she called out, feeling a solid sense of purpose supplant her weariness. "Private, get my supplies! We're late!"

Quickly she finished her morning prayers, giving thanks to God for the miracles He had worked during the night. Soon the horse—which, to her great surprise, was the runaway mare—and the aide were ready. Once in the saddle, she charged off toward the front, as she had done so many times before, praying to be led to those in greatest need. The aide trailed behind, calling for her to slow down, yet she pressed on.

Another day had begun.

Deviled eggs?" Meg called out.

"Got 'em," Tyler shouted back. "Mom, everything's in the car. Let's get going."

"What about napkins?"

"They're right here. Come on, we're gonna be late."

Meg raced for the door. Passing the hall mirror, she paused and swept back her blonde hair—okay, she'd highlighted it to hide the gray, but she was pleased at how young she still looked. A quick flip of an elastic band, and she flounced out of the house, ponytail swinging.

"Did you remember the lawn chairs?" she asked her husband as she slipped into the passenger side of their minivan. "I don't know, for some reason I'm nervous about this picnic. Do you think we're forgetting something?"

"My mind!" Tyler said from the backseat. "Oh no, I've lost my mind."

"Ha-ha, very funny." Meg flipped open the mirror on the sun visor and checked her lipstick as

Dan pulled out into the street. "You're not the one who had to organize all the details for this shindig, Tyler. I don't know why Charlie's mom wanted to hold it on a Sunday. I worried all the way through Bible study and church this morning. Four graduating seniors and their friends and families—who knows how many people are going to show up? What if we don't have enough food?"

"I'll just run over to KFC and pick up some extra boxes of chicken," Dan said.

"I hope Jake and Martha can find the park."

"I drew a map at the ceremony yesterday. They'll be okay."

"Hey, Mom," Tyler spoke up. "Uncle Jake said he gave you an old Civil War letter signed by Major General Maxwell. Is that for real?"

Meg pursed her lips for a moment, recalling the incredible bravery of her son's ancestor. Elizabeth Rogers had later married Alden Chilton, and their blood flowed through Tyler's veins.

"It appears to be Maxwell's signature," she said.

"That's amazing. How did Uncle Jake get the letter?"

"He found it among *Grandmaman* Solange's papers. It was sent to your great-great-great-grandmother after the war. When Major General Maxwell was wounded during battle in Chancellorsville, Virginia, she saved his life."

"Was she a nurse or something?"

"Yes, but she went far beyond her medical duties. She disguised herself in a dead soldier's uniform and acted as a decoy to draw the enemy away from the general."

"Wow." He fell silent. "That was pretty smart thinking."

Meg stared down at her picnic list and tried to focus on the myriad details remaining. But it was impossible to keep her thoughts from the amazing courage of a simple woman, alone on a bloody battlefield and surrounded by enemies. How had Elizabeth summoned the courage to shed the security of her identity as a woman? Why had she been willing to give her life for a man she had never met before?

More than bravery, Elizabeth's actions had proven the value of her high intelligence. Only someone with a combination of those two qualities could have succeeded in such a precarious situation. Meg had to admit her assertion that Tyler was too smart for the military wasn't exactly valid. In fact, wartime called on men and women to have common sense, quick wits, strategic skill, and just about every kind of mental prowess humans possess.

"So, Mom," Tyler said, and Meg cringed, almost certain of what was to follow. "My great-to-the-umpteenth-power grandma carried a message for a dead Revolutionary War soldier—at the risk of losing her first child. And my nearly-as-many-greats grandma in the Civil War had the brains and the courage to figure out how to save a general's life. And you don't think I should have the same chance to do something important for our country?"

Meg glanced at Dan for help. Her husband was staring straight ahead, his jaw tight.

"Tyler, can we please not talk about this right now?" she asked. "I want to make sure the picnic comes off well."

"I want to make sure my *life* comes off well, Mom. I want to do what God is leading me to do. You and Dad have been my spiritual authority for eighteen years. Are you going to go against God's will now?"

"God's specific will can be very difficult to pin-point, honey," Meg said. "We know that, in general, His will is that we obey Him and lead others to Him. But as for the details . . . well, we pray, of course, and we search the Scripture for answers. Basically, though, God leads us according to the way He's shaped our lives. We don't rely on our feelings. We look at evidence. God has given you a happy, two-parent home, a good education, an excellent mind and body—and He's given you the opportunity to advance yourself by studying at one of the finest universities in America. Every arrow in your life points to *that* future as being God's will, Tyler. Can you see what I'm saying?"

"Yeah, but if what you're saying were true, there wouldn't have been a Lottie Moon or Adoniram Judson or Bill Wallace—or any of the other missionaries we learned about in church. God had those people brought up by regular, average parents in podunk towns. All the arrows would have pointed them toward marriage, settling down, holding ordinary jobs, and having families. But they didn't follow the arrows because they felt God calling them to do something that didn't seem to make sense—and yet, it was right. It was the right thing to go out to China or India or wherever. Can you see what *I'm* saying?"

"God isn't calling you to be a missionary, Tyler."

"No, He's calling me to serve in the Army. What makes one calling more right than another? It would be okay if I wanted to be a missionary in China but not to help defend the freedom of the United States?"

"China is not open to missionaries," Meg said.

Tyler thumped the back of her headrest. "Mom, you're not listening to me!"

"Yes, I am. I'm trying very hard to hear you and to understand your point of view. But what you see as God's calling, I see as the valley of the shadow of death. And I don't want you to go there!"

"Why not? The Bible tells us to fear no evil in that valley. I'm not afraid, you know. So, why won't you give me your blessing?"

"I'll tell you why not . . . because I'm your mother, that's why not." The knot in her throat tightened. "I love you, Tyler. I want you to be safe and happy. I don't want you to throw away this incredible opportunity just because some recruiter dropped by the high school and gave you a pep talk."

"Mom!"

"That's enough, you two," Dan cut in. "Let's drop this subject now, and I mean it. We're here at the park to celebrate Tyler's graduation and to have fun with our family and friends. None of us knows what the future will bring anyway. Let's give the topic a rest."

"Fine," Meg said as her husband pulled into a parking space near the open-air pavilion. "That's fine with me. I wish the whole thing had never come up. And you can forget about me signing off on this, Tyler, because it's not going to happen."

"I didn't ask for your permission," he said. "I asked for your blessing."

The door slammed behind him, and he was off at a brisk jog toward a cluster of his friends near the soft-drink cooler. Dan turned off the engine and let out a breath.

"I'm going to give him my blessing, Meg," he

said. "Tyler's an adult now. There's nothing we can do."

"He's not an adult. He'll still be a teenager for nearly two more years! Oh, Dan, please stand beside me in this. I don't want him to make a mistake he'll regret for the rest of his life."

"If we don't give him our blessing, Meg, he may resent us for the rest of his life."

She sniffed back the tears that threatened. "That would be *his* choice."

"You're that sure he's wrong about God calling him to the military?"

"I don't know," she whispered. "I hardly know what's right or wrong anymore. I just don't want my son . . . my baby . . . to go off to some foreign land and die. I couldn't stand it, Dan. He's all we have."

"It would do us both in to lose him. But we don't know that he would ever be called on to fight, Meg. He might be assigned to communications or supplies or something completely safe."

"You know I'm not just talking about the dangers of battle. These days our enemies are using chemicals and bioterrorism. Those things won't affect just the front line. And even if he never faces an enemy, there's such a risk of him straying from the Lord, Dan. You were a soldier. You know the temptations."

"I do." He shook his head. "But we can't protect him forever. He's all grown-up now."

"Is he? Look at him standing over there, so tall and self-assured. But I remember when he was nursing . . . crawling across the floors on his chubby little knees . . . and scuffing up the toes of those tiny suede walking shoes he had. Remember, Dan? Remember that?"

"Yeah, I do."

"It was yesterday that you held him in your arms and rocked him to sleep. Doesn't it seem that way? Like you two were just out in the backyard building his tree house. Like I just finished sewing his little corduroy overalls with the bunny buttons. It's as though the time went by too fast, and he's not ready."

"*You're* not ready, Meg. Tyler's ready." He squeezed her hand. "Tyler's had a good mom, and you got him ready for the big wide world. Now it's up to him to choose which way he's going to go."

A knock on the window drew Meg's attention.

Jake grinned through the glass. "No crying allowed at the picnic, Meg!" her brother-in-law admonished as she stepped out of the car. "Come on, let's unpack this trunk. The young'uns are startin' to howl."

Stuffing away her hurt and frustration, Meg helped in unloading the car and arranging the long buffet table. Charlie's mother was hard at work hanging balloons and a big banner across the pavilion. The other parents had brought barbecued beef, hamburgers, hot dogs, and enough potato salad, deviled eggs, baked beans, and coleslaw to feed the crowd twice over. And that didn't include the array of chocolate cakes, pecan pies, and blackberry cobblers that lined the dessert table.

After the prayer, everyone sat down to eat. Meg found a place near Dan and tried to join in the conversation around her. Everyone was so jolly, celebrating the achievements of the four young graduates. But all Meg could think about was her refusal to bless her son. How cruel she must seem to Tyler, and how impossible it must be for him to understand her refusal to support his decision.

Could he be right in his understanding of

God's will? Would the Lord really ask for the life of Tyler Chilton? In spite of the May heat, Meg shivered. Lately, she had been too upset by her son's announcement and too busy with plans for his graduation to spend much time in the Bible. What did God's Word really say about war and the sacrifice of precious sons?

As she picked at her potato salad, Meg recalled how God had commanded Abraham to take his son Isaac up a mountain and kill him on an altar. Then she thought of Hannah, who had given her only son, Samuel, to serve all his life in God's temple. Now that she focused on it, she could remember a lot of sons who had been killed—Abel was murdered at the hand of his brother; Samson was crushed under the Philistine temple; all of Job's children died when a wind blew their house down; Saul's son Jonathan was killed in a battle with the Philistines; David's son Absalom got his head stuck in a tree and was slain by Joab and his armor bearers—and those were just the ones Meg could remember.

Of course, there was one Son who stood out from the rest. God Himself had been willing to sacrifice His only child—sending Him to the most foreign of places to die the cruelest of deaths. Meg gazed down at her chocolate meringue pie and felt guiltier than ever.

She tried to tell herself that these stories of sacrifice didn't compare to her own situation. She wasn't a pillar of faith like Job. She wasn't royalty like David. And she certainly wasn't God. She was just average Meg Chilton who loved her only son and wanted to see him safely off to Yale. Was that so bad?

"Hey, Mom, you look like you ate a worm or something." Tyler slung his arm around her as he slid onto the picnic bench at her side. "You okay?"

She mustered a smile. "Just thinking about everything. I feel so awful about all this, Tyler. About the arguing. About not being able to give you my blessing. I've always tried to affirm everything you've chosen to do. I've been behind you all the way."

"I know. That's why this feels so weird. You're my cheerleader, my biggest fan."

"Rah, rah."

"I'm not trying to hurt you with this decision,

Mom. I'm trying to do what I believe God is leading me to do. Yale would be great—but it's all about me. The Army—that's about something important."

"You're important, Tyler," Meg said. "You're important to your dad and me. And not only to us. You know the family tree I've been working on since you were a freshman?"

"Believe me, I know. I've been hearing about dead relatives till I'm about ready to scream."

"Those 'dead relatives' include some amazing people. And you're the only link to them."

"What do you mean?"

"You're the last in the Chilton line. There are other branches going off one way or another. But in your father's direct line, you're the only one left."

He gave her a squeeze. "That's cool, Mom. But everybody's got a genealogy, you know."

"Yes, but you're the last to bear the family name. It almost ended once before, you know, during the First World War. There were two Chilton boys left to carry on the line, and they both went to battle. The oldest, Henry, was killed, and the other . . . well, if Willis Chilton hadn't done what he did, that would have been the end of it. You never would have been born. We're at that point on the chart again, Tyler. There are two Chilton men left: your dad and Uncle Jake. Jake and Martha don't have children. The Chilton lineage can only continue through you."

"Are you saying I'm supposed to stay alive, get married, and have sons just so I can make that chart in your office longer?"

"No, Tyler, but—"

"Mom, the way you think, only orphans ought to be soldiers." He brushed a quick kiss across her cheek. "Lighten up. It's not the family tree that really matters, is it? It's what the people on your chart did with their lives. That's what counts."

"But lineage is important. The Bible is full of lists of 'begats'—"

"Yeah, and those are the parts I always skip." He swung his long legs over the bench. "Hey, Charlie and some of the guys are coming over to watch videos and play games tonight. Is that okay?"

"Sure!" *I love it when you and your friends are in the basement,* she wanted to say. *I love the smells of pizza and popcorn, the sounds of laughter and electronics, even the sticky messes*

I have to wade through in the morning or the hundred soda cans I have to pick up. I love everything about you, Tyler Chilton—everything you do and say and think is precious to me. You are my beloved son in whom I am well pleased.

As he sauntered off to join his friends, a prayer swelled in Meg's chest. *Lord, I love him so much. He's my only child. He's my precious, adored son. He's the last in the line of this wonderful, brave Chilton family. Please, dear God, don't ask me to sacrifice him!*

She closed her eyes, wondering how Cornelia Chilton must have felt knowing that her children—her two precious sons, the last of the Chiltons—were huddled in the trenches of German-held France, the stench of mustard gas all around them and the burst of mortar shells ringing in their ears. . . .

Argonne Forest, France
October 1918

"You're looking a little bleary-eyed this morning, Willy-boy. Did those whizbangs interrupt your beauty rest?"

"I'd venture to say a night of artillery fire doesn't suit your constitution, either," Willis Chilton quipped, a tired grin creasing his face as he regarded his older brother, Henry, in the gray light of dawn. Both men had dark circles etched in the skin beneath their eyes.

Here near the front, the noise never stopped. Airplanes growled and snarled overhead, engaging in duels of their own when they weren't strafing and bombing the ground below. Machine-gun and artillery fire were ceaseless. The worst thing about the shelling, Willis had decided long ago, was living with the constant dread of wondering when and where the missiles were going to fall. He had seen more than one man made suddenly into mincemeat.

As a part of Major General John Pershing's newly created American First Army, the brothers' company was encamped in the tangled woods of the Meuse-Argonne sector of France. The objective of their offensive was to secure the Argonne Forest and to push the Germans back past the Sedan-Mézières rail line before winter set in. It would be no easy task. The enemy had occupied this area for four years and were well entrenched.

A shell hit a few hundred yards to the south, its concussion causing the muddy ground on which they stood to shudder.

"Whizbang, bang, bang," Henry remarked with false cheer. His blue eyes were steady. Beneath his helmet, close-cropped, russet-colored hair complemented his strong, rugged face.

"What do they say . . . there's no rest for the tired?"

"Wicked," Willis supplied with a chuckle. "They say there's no rest for the wicked."

"Well, I'm not wicked; I'm just plumb worn out. How 'bout you, little brother? How're you holding up?"

"Just fine. Willing and ready to go to the limit if that's God's plan for my life."

Henry nodded, approval and tenderness shining from his gaze. "You've always given your all, Willy. You do the Lord and our family proud. Not to mention our country."

"Me?" Willis shook his head and gave his brother a punch on the arm. "Look who's talking."

Henry shrugged. "Hey, beef and boiled spuds this morning. Hot food . . . a real treat. You coming?"

Willis waved him off. "I'll be along in a few minutes."

"You'd better hope I don't eat it all up."

Willis laughed and watched his older brother start toward the mess tent. Henry's broad shoulders filled out his uniform. His stride was sure and graceful, Willis observed, and he possessed an aura of confidence that made him a natural leader.

Thank You for allowing us to be here together, Willis prayed silently as he watched Henry stoop to enter the tent. All his life he had been profoundly grateful to have such a brother to look up to. Some big brothers might chafe at having an adoring younger brother underfoot, but Henry had never been that way. From Willis's earliest memories, Henry had been a most willing teacher, mentor, protector, and friend.

And if anyone did the Chilton family proud, it was Henry. Whether in academics, athletics, music, morals, or character, Henry Chilton always outshone his competition. Since his arrival in France, he had proven his bravery countless times, receiving commendation for his courage in rescuing wounded soldiers trapped in the perilous no-man's-land between opposing lines. Just yesterday he had been responsible for wiping out an enemy machine-gun nest.

Willis knew that Henry's wife, Lorna Mae, worried dreadfully about her husband's safety. The joyful date of their wedding had coincided with the sinking of the British passenger liner *Lusitania*. Nearly two years after that day, President Woodrow Wilson announced a state of war between the United States and Germany. By that time, Lorna Mae was expecting their second child.

Rather than be drafted, Henry chose to volunteer. Willis, a bachelor, was of the same mind. Together they enlisted, were trained, and sent abroad. Outraged by the bold, predatory tactics of the Germans, their hearts burned with the zeal to fight for the sake of righteousness. Today that zeal was still there, Willis reflected, but tempered by the harsh, ugly realities of war.

All too soon it was time to pull on his coat and sling his rifle over his shoulder. The muddy ground upon which their division had advanced the day before was strewn with unburied dead, a distressingly common sight.

"Got a letter from Lorna Mae," Henry reported, catching up to walk beside Willis in a place where the trees were wider apart. He patted his pocket as they marched and smiled broadly. "She wrote that Mabel just took her first steps."

"I suppose we'll be hearing about this for days to come now." Willis couldn't resist teasing his brother, for everyone who knew Henry knew how dear his wife and daughters were to him.

"She's also saying *hot* and *no-no.*"

"Well, if you'd only do your part, Chilton," joshed Freeport, the banty-legged private ahead of them, "we could hurry up and go home before she starts reciting the Gettysburg Address." His boots, like theirs, sucked into the muddy ground with each step.

"True, he's got a ways to go to live up to our grandmother's military reputation," Willis mischievously chipped in.

"Grandmother?" Freeport's expression was quizzical. "What's that you say—"

The screaming of a mortar shell interrupted his words, and they immediately crouched down, trying to make themselves the smallest targets possible. The ensuing explosion rained muck and shards of wood over them, but they were unharmed.

"Time for work." Henry stood and shook himself off, all business now.

Before long, they were again in the thick of battle. Unlike the swift advance the First Army had made in the Saint-Mihiel offensive the previous month, their momentum was now greatly hampered by the difficult terrain. This morning their goal was to capture the hill that rose before them, a challenging feat due to the German superior position.

A hail of enemy machine-gun fire sent Willis behind a tree. Breathing hard, his back pressed against the rough trunk, he looked around for Henry. His brother was in a similar position a dozen yards to his right. Henry nodded to him.

Then, as he often did, Henry charged suddenly from his position, aiming for the protection of a tree ahead. In disbelief and horror, Willis watched his brother's head snap back violently. His sturdy body arced backward into the air, then crumpled to the ground.

"No!" Without thought of danger, Willis raced

to his brother's side. At once he knew Henry was dead. Time seemed to stand motionless as he stared into the face that he loved more dearly than his own. The sights and sounds about him withdrew to the periphery of his awareness. He sank to his hands and knees.

Henry was dead? He said the words to himself. *Henry is dead.* They didn't make sense. Neither did it make sense that so many men fighting for the cause of freedom could be turned into so many corpses. It simply wasn't real. The bullet hole in Henry's forehead couldn't be real.

As if someone else controlled his hands, Willis watched as others opened Henry's breast pocket and removed the letter that had just arrived from his wife, as well as the sealed envelope behind it. The second was a letter from Henry to Lorna Mae, to be given to her in the event of his death.

Something shuddered inside Willis, a foretaste of the intense mourning that was to come, he imagined, although he continued to hover in a state of disbelief. "Oh, dear God," came a choking prayer from his throat, but it ended there. He could not go on. What could he say?

A sudden, excruciating pain in his arm multiplied his bewilderment, as did the muddy ground rushing up to meet his face.

Many months later, after stays in a series of hospitals, Willis had finally returned to his parents' home. He knew now that his left humerus had been shattered by a bullet that also had pierced his lung, and that a fragment of bone had opened an artery in his upper arm. If not for the courage of Jimmy Freeport, who had risked his life to pull Willis to safety, he would have bled to death beside Henry. He remembered nothing about the ambulance ride or the field hospital, but the queer image of a nurse in boots and a raincoat lingered in his mind from his indistinct memories of being at the evacuation hospital.

When he had finally been ready for discharge, the doctors told him his damaged arm would never function normally. It was with grim satisfaction that through hard work, he'd been able to prove them at least partly wrong. Yet though his bones had knit and his wounds healed into scars, his heart was much slower to mend. Even now, his mind's eye could recall Henry's death with disturbing clarity. The grief he carried, once so paralyzing that he prayed for death, was lifting in slow layers.

"Uncle Willis! Uncle Willis!" His niece Pearl's bright call interrupted his thoughts. From her front porch she bounded to meet him on the sidewalk and threw herself into his waiting arms. Last summer he had been too weak to lift his nieces, much less walk the six blocks from his parents' home to Lorna Mae's. This summer he was able to do both, and he frequently did after finishing his day's work at the factory. Pearl, now four years old, looped her arms about his neck and kissed his cheek. Her weight in his arms and the clean, little-child smell of her hair tugged painfully at his heart, making him aware that he was enjoying something of Henry's that Henry could not.

As he carried Pearl up the front path, Lorna Mae came out the door, two-year-old Mabel on her heels. The door squeaked louder than it had two days earlier, and he made a mental note to oil the hinges and check the screws before he returned home.

"Good evening, Willis." Lorna Mae greeted him with her lovely, quiet smile. She was much thinner than she had been before the war, and her eyes still carried the shadow of her grief. He recalled the day last summer when he'd given her the letter Henry had written. She had received it with such dignity. And then after reading her husband's words, she had shared the letter with his parents and with Willis.

Loving. Giving. Generous. Beautiful inside as well as out. Oh yes, Henry had known what he was doing when he set about winning the heart of Lorna Mae McConnell. On their wedding day, Willis remembered thinking that Henry had never looked happier. Now more than ever it was evident that the elder Chilton had chosen well, for his widow was determined to carry on bravely for the sake of their daughters. Lorna Mae frequently said that she chose to trust in the Lord's provision for the fatherless and the widowed.

"Do you want some cake, Uncle Willis?" Pearl entreated. "We made you a spice cake today."

"We make cake!" Mabel seconded, clapping her hands.

"I have a few things to do, and then I would be happy to have some of your cake," he replied. "I sure hope there's a pitcher of lemonade to go with it," he added as he set Pearl down on the porch.

"There is!" she burst out. "I helped make it, and it's very good."

"You're *sure* it's good? Cutting grass is thirsty work, you understand."

While both girls clamored to tell him how delicious their goodies were, Lorna Mae smiled at Willis over their heads and thanked him for his help. Somehow that smile lightened his chores and his spirit, and while he mowed, he found himself humming. Though he knew she regarded him as Henry's younger brother, it was becoming altogether too commonplace for his thoughts of Lorna Mae to border on the romantic.

Dusk was falling, and the girls had been tucked into bed by the time he finished the half-dozen chores he'd come over to do. Lorna Mae had a generous wedge of cake ready for him on the arm of the porch swing. With satisfaction, he finished every morsel of the tasty dessert, washing it down with a glass of icy lemonade.

"Lorna Mae Chilton, that was the most delicious cake I believe I have ever eaten."

"Are you hinting for another slice?"

He delighted in the lilt of her voice as she took his dishes. "No, thank you. That was just right."

A few moments later she returned, taking a seat at the other end of the swing. Together they rocked in silence while the summer darkness deepened.

"I miss Henry," she said softly after a time.

"I do too." At the memory of seeing his brother fall, Willis felt his throat grow tight.

"Willis?"

With difficulty, he swallowed. "Yes?"

"It must have been difficult for you over there."

"Yes."

"I'm sorry." Her dress rustled as she slid closer to him.

"God was good enough to give me Henry's company," he finally said. There was so much he would never tell her. The trenches, the mud, the rats. The incessant bombing, the fear, the sights and smells of human death and putrefaction . . . the helpless soul sickness of wondering how many men he had killed.

"Willis?"

"Yes?" An electric shock went through him as

she moved closer still. The smell of her lavender fragrance mingled with the summer night's perfume of fresh-mown grass.

"Will you hold my hand?" she whispered.

"I . . . I—" Before he knew what to say, her small hand had found its way into his.

"You've been very good to us."

"I-it's . . . the least I can do for you and the girls," he stammered, feeling his heart bump oddly within his chest. "Henry was the hero. I'm just . . . well, I'm just an ordinary fellow."

"Do you truly believe that a man who cares faithfully for his late brother's family without asking anything in return is ordinary?"

A self-deprecating chuckle left him. "Yes, ordinary. I'm nowhere near the man Henry—"

"Hush, Willis Chilton," Lorna Mae interrupted, her gentle voice ringing with emotion. "You're a wonderful man in your own right."

Without quite knowing how it happened, Henry let go of Lorna Mae's hand and placed his arm protectively around her slender shoulders. They trembled with her weeping, adding to the tenderness he already felt for her. He wanted nothing more than to protect her from every bit of hurt and suffering the world held.

"Shhh," he soothed. "We both miss him."

"You know I loved my husband with my whole heart."

"I know you did. And he loved you the same, Lorna Mae. All he ever did over there was talk about you. You and the girls."

"Willis," she finally said, retrieving a hanky and wiping her eyes, "I want to tell you something."

"You don't have to thank me for—"

"No. I wasn't going to thank you. I want to say . . . I think . . ." She paused and took a deep breath. "Willis, I believe . . . I am falling in love with you."

Of all the things Lorna Mae Chilton might have told him, this was the one he least expected. His heart lurched crazily. Had he heard her correctly? She was falling in love with . . . *him?* It couldn't be true, yet here she was, so beautiful and sweet, in his arms.

"Oh, I'm sorry, Willis, for shocking you," she went on. "But I thought if I didn't tell you, you would never look at me except as a sister. You're too much a gentleman."

"I daren't look at you, Lorna Mae," he admitted in a low voice. "Because if I did, you would know how I felt about you. And I just didn't think that would be right."

A long moment passed while they rocked beneath the eaves. A dog barked somewhere, then was quiet.

Finally, Lorna Mae spoke. "This autumn, Henry will be gone two years. Before he left, he told me that if he didn't come back, he would want me to love again. For a long time, I didn't think it was possible. But now, Willis—"

"Do you know what you're saying?" he heard himself interrupt. "Because I'll marry you tomorrow, if that's what you want." He lifted her fingers and kissed the back of her hand. "And as your husband, I promise to cherish you for all the rest of my days. I'll love and provide for your daughters as I would my own."

"I know you will," she said, turning her face up toward his. "And if God is willing, it would give me such joy to bear your children. I pray that He might bless us with a son to carry on the Chilton name. Family was so important to Henry, and it is to you too."

Willis was silent, touched more deeply than he could ever recall. "Yes," he said slowly, feeling a lightness—a hope—grow in his heart. "A son would be an incredible gift."

"Now that we've discussed the family we hope to have, does this mean we're courting?" she asked, offering her lips.

"Oh yes," he replied, rejoicing in the sweetness of her kiss and the warmth of her embrace. "We are, indeed. I love you, Lorna Mae. But I am wondering one thing . . ."

"What is it?"

"If I marry you, will I get cake and kisses every day?"

"If you like, Mr. Chilton," she said coyly.

"Well, I suppose I could settle for just the cake," he teased, chuckling at her gasp of feigned outrage. "But I'd be a fool if I didn't take both."

Meg studied the small medal in the palm of her hand. A Purple Heart. With it, a letter of commendation. Accolades of every kind. But these had been awarded to a dead man.

Henry Chilton had been killed in World War I, and his younger brother, Willis, was left to carry on without his beloved sibling and boyhood idol. Willis Chilton had been a brave man, but Meg couldn't help wondering what use courage was when you were forced to go on living without someone you loved.

And how had their mother, Cornelia Chilton, felt? Willis wasn't the "spare child" who could take Henry's place in his mother's heart. Both boys must have been special to her. Each one a miracle. Cornelia surely suffered great agony when both her boys went off to fight in Europe. She must have known they carried with them the family name and all hope for its future. Henry had left two daughters, and Willis wasn't married. And yet, she let them go.

Had she done this gladly? bravely? Or had she fought it, like Meg continued to do?

In the two days following the graduation picnic, Meg had thrown herself into her work. Avoiding all mention of the issue of Tyler's determination to enlist in the Army, she focused on daily life—dusting; laundering a mountain of blue jeans, T-shirts, and dirty socks; creating sketches for her new line of floral fabrics. When she found spare time on her hands, she retreated to her home office and dug around in her genealogy files.

Even though Meg had decided not to give Tyler the journal she had so carefully penned, she was drawn again and again to the small envelope filled with information about Henry Chilton and his younger brother, Willis. Quiet and unassuming, Willis had followed his much-admired sibling into the trenches of France, and there he had watched Henry die.

Willis had been willing to go, to sacrifice his own life if necessary, and to carry on after his brother was killed. So why couldn't Meg be as brave? Though Willis had been wounded, he hadn't left nearly the military legacy that his brother had. A plain and simple man, he simply had gone on about the business of living. But the inner core of strength that had led Willis to France had also led him to care for his brother's widow and daughters, to lead an exemplary Christian life, and to build the family that carried on the Chilton legacy.

Only one fragile document remained to mark the life of Willis Chilton. Meg drew the eulogy from the envelope and read again the words carefully composed by his wife, Lorna Mae. Though she had initially chosen Henry over his younger brother and had borne her first husband two daughters, years later Lorna Mae wrote of her deep love for her second husband—a man whose kindness, courage, and loyalty had characterized his life.

"Hey, Mom?" Tyler poked his head through the door into her office. "I've gotta run a few errands—return some movies, pick up my grades, stuff like that. Do you need anything from downtown?"

Meg slipped the eulogy back into the file and laid it on her desk. "You could mail this letter for me. I've written to ask for the service records of your great-grandfather, Willis Chilton."

"World War . . . One?"

"Good!" She smiled at her son. "You're getting the hang of this."

"I'll never know them as well as you do."

"I've learned a lot by studying these people. Not just names, either. Willis married his brother's widow; did you realize that? If he hadn't, there would have been no more Chiltons. Willis didn't earn a chest full of medals like Henry, but he was just as brave. I want to see if I can find out more about his years of service. He was wounded, but there's only a brief mention of it in his eulogy."

"Does Dad know anything about him?"

"Your father was ten when Willis Chilton died. Like a good grandpa, he used to prop your dad on his knee and tell all kinds of stories about the past. But Willis rarely spoke of the war years. I'm not sure he ever really got over the death of his brother."

Tyler gazed down at the carpet, the toe of one enormous shoe nudging at a fabric scrap on the floor. "Sometimes I wish I had a brother."

"I know, sweetie. But with your father's health so bad after Vietnam—"

"Yeah, I know—I'm the miracle baby." He gave

her that shy grin she loved so well. "Speaking of Dad, he . . . uh . . . he talked to me this morning after breakfast. He gave me his blessing to enlist."

Meg looked away. "He told me he intended to do that."

"Are you mad at him?"

"No."

"At me?"

"No."

"Well . . . while I'm downtown, I thought I'd drop by the office. You know, where the recruiters work?"

"By the Dairy Queen."

"Uh-huh. So, anyway . . . well . . . I'm going to go ahead and sign up."

Meg fingered the corner of the Willis Chilton envelope, unable to bring herself to speak. She had felt this way once before. When her mother had died, Meg was only fifteen. As the pallbearers carried the casket out of the hearse, she had clenched her fists in pent-up rage.

No! she'd wanted to scream. *No, stop this! Stop this from happening. I don't want this to be true. Everything is going to be different and horrible. Make it stop!*

"Mom?" Tyler took a step toward her. "Have you thought any more about giving me your blessing?"

Should I give you my blessing to go away, to vanish, to put yourself in a place of destruction, desolation, and death? Should I lay my hand on my dear son, my only child, and bless him in his desire to tear himself from safety and security, and to throw himself in the path of danger?

"I've thought about it," she managed. "I've come to realize that even though you're the last of the Chiltons, the family name isn't as important as the character and courage of the people who wear it."

"That's right, Mom."

"And I've thought about all the women who willingly sacrificed their children to military service. Even the ones who had only one child. A really smart child. I want to be like them. I want to have the courage to do this."

"Do you think you can, Mom? I have to be obedient to God's will. I have to go where He leads me. Can you give me your blessing to do that?" He shifted from one foot to the other. "It would mean a lot to me."

Somewhere deep in her heart, his plea echoed and reverberated. And then she heard a responding cry as the words of Jesus rang out: *"If you want to be My follower you must love Me more than your own father and mother, wife and children, brothers and sisters—yes, more than your own life. Otherwise, you cannot be My disciple."*

"No," she whispered, choking on her tears.

"What?" Tyler said. "Did you say something?"

Again, the voice of Scripture blew through her spirit: *"I assure you . . . everyone who has given up houses or brothers or sisters or father or mother or children or property, for My sake, will receive a hundred times as much in return and will have eternal life."*

"I don't want to—" Meg reached for a tissue— "I don't care about reward. I'm ashamed of myself, but I just . . . I just can't do it."

A third time, the voice of the Spirit rocketed through her: *"If you love your son or daughter more than Me, you are not worthy of being Mine. If you refuse to take up your cross and follow Me, you are not worthy of being Mine. If you cling to your life, you will lose it; but if you give it up for Me, you will find it."*

Meg sucked down a sob. "I know what's right, Tyler. I know you hear God speaking to you, and I should let you follow Him. I ought to give you my blessing. In my heart, I feel sure of what I have to do. But I just can't."

"Why not, Mom? Why is it so hard?"

"I love you too much, Tyler. I just love you . . . too much."

"Is that possible?"

"Yes, and I know it's wrong. I should be obedient to the Holy Spirit. But I'm just a sinful . . . plain old . . . selfish mother."

"I've never thought of you as selfish, Mom. You've always given and given. Every time I needed something, you made sure I had it. You always put yourself last. Dad would say the same thing."

"Well, he would be wrong." Meg blotted her cheeks. "Maybe it looked like I was putting you and Dad first, but you're both a part of me. And in that way, I was meeting my own needs. Now it's time— all the books I've read about the 'empty nest' say it's time—to separate from you, Tyler. You're supposed to go off and be your own person, apart from me. But I've spent eighteen years loving you, feeling your every ache, drying your every tear, longing for the fulfillment of your every dream.

The umbilical cord might as well still be hanging there between us."

"That's gross, Mom."

"Yeah, well, it may be gross, but it's true. I have done a lousy, terrible job of preparing myself to turn you out of this cozy little womb of ours. Now you not only want to leave, but you want to head straight into the darkest, deepest valley you can find. Can't you just go to Yale? Please?"

Tyler stared at her, his blue eyes soft. "God told me to enlist in the Army."

"Oh, Tyler!"

"Look, I know you love me, but all the other guys in the military have moms who love them too. You can't send just the unloved ones to war. The unwanted ones. It's the sons and boyfriends and husbands who have to go, Mom. It's daughters and wives too. Those they leave behind are asked to make that sacrifice . . . to say, 'I love you, and I'm letting you go.' "

She shook her head and blew her nose into a tissue. "I can't. I just can't do it. I'm too weak."

"What's going on here?" Dan emerged from the stairwell. "Meg, you okay?"

"No," she sobbed. "I'm not okay. Nothing is okay. I feel like I'm dying inside. I know I'm going against God's will, and it's so wrong. But I can't give up my son. I just can't do it, Dan."

Her husband stepped to her side and wrapped Meg in his arms. "You've always been a good mom. A great wife and mother."

"But this is . . . so hard. Too hard."

"I don't see why it's such a big deal to Mom," Tyler said to his father. "I'm leaving home anyway. I'm just taking a different path than we'd planned."

"It's a big deal because *you're* a big deal, Tyler." Dan reached out and rumpled his son's hair. "You won't understand until you're a father. You may never understand the depth of our love for you, unless you're in the same boat we were in so many years ago. I nearly died in 'Nam—malaria was rampant over there in the jungle, you know. I ran such a high temperature, the docs thought I might be brain-dead. I was even in a coma for a while, and they figured I'd never recover. But I fought my way back—every bit as rough a battle as the one I'd been fighting with my gun. Finally I recovered, and things pretty much got back to normal."

"I don't think you've ever really recovered, honey," Meg said, squeezing her husband's hand. "Your dad still suffers relapses of the malarial fevers, Tyler. I'm not sure you knew that. He was so strong and tough before he went off to Vietnam. We dated through high school, even though we met when he was a senior and I was just a freshman. I waited for him all those years, praying every day that he'd come back to me safe and sound. And then . . . there he was!"

Dan chuckled. "Scrawny as a plucked chicken, yellow from head to toe, and about as cynical as a boy can get. But she loved me anyhow, and we got married right off the bat. We waited a while to start trying to have children—got ourselves established first, got me a job, bought this house, you know."

"And then when we felt it was time to start a family," Meg said, gazing into her husband's deep blue eyes, "we couldn't."

"Took us a few good years to figure out that the malarial fever had left me pretty much sterilized. Finally the docs just told us to give it up because it wasn't going to happen. By then, your mom was getting toward the age where it can be dangerous for women to have babies, and we decided to let it go. But we sure did want a child. We prayed morning and night; we cried lots of times. Well, your mom did, anyway. And the years just kept ticking by. Then one day she got as sick as an ol' dog. We thought it was the flu—but it was you!"

Meg smiled and shivered, recalling vividly the moment when the doctor had burst into the waiting room to tell her the good news. "We could hardly believe it, but it was true. I was pregnant! And seven months later, you were born. Our precious gift from God. Our miracle."

"So don't be too rough on your mom, Tyler," Dan said. "It's hard for any parent to let their young one leave the nest. It's even harder when the child is going into the military. But for us . . . well, it's that much more difficult. Not because we never thought we'd have a baby, but because once we did, our love was so strong."

"Okay, you guys are freaking me out a little bit here," Tyler said. "I mean, every kid wants to be loved, but this is . . . like . . . too much."

"We're not trying to overwhelm you with the story," Meg assured him. "We've tried never to be overpossessive with you or make you feel like your life has to be enmeshed with ours. I think Dad told you the story because we want you to understand why it's so hard. We want you to see things through our eyes a little bit."

"I do." He hung his head. "I understand, and I'm sorry to hurt you so much. But you're also the ones who taught me to follow Christ. I love you guys, but I love Him more. And this is something I have to do—because He said so."

Silence fell across the little office. Dan's arm tightened around Meg as she clutched his hand.

Finally, Tyler let out a breath. "Well, I've gotta run those errands," he said. "All of them."

Before Meg could speak, he was off, thundering down the stairs and banging the back screen door as he ran out to his car. As the sound of his car receded through the open window, Meg shuddered.

"There's another story you ought to know," Dan said. "It's about my brother."

"Has something happened to Jake?" Alarm stiffened Meg's back. "What's wrong?"

"He's fine. It's just that I have some genealogy information for you."

"What do you mean, Dan?"

"There's sort of . . . well, kind of a family secret. It's not a bad thing, really. It's just not something we think about much. Or discuss. But maybe it'll help you understand the kind of heart that beats inside your son's chest. The courage and strength and determination that flow through his veins. This is a story about what true love really means."

Meg stared at her husband. "Tell me, Dan. Tell me everything."

"The story starts with my dad, Irving Kent Chilton. You know, he wasn't much of a looker after he got that scar on his face."

Meg nodded, recalling the incongruity of Irving Chilton, his face disfigured from an accident in his teens, standing beside his beautiful war bride, Solange. Meg had also been disturbed by the fact that Dan's brother Jake's birth date barely followed the date of their parents' wedding. Did Solange truly love the scarred Irving, whom she had met in France during the Battle of the Bulge? What didn't Meg know about Irving Chilton?

"I can still remember my father telling me about Pearl Harbor," Dan said. "He was a young, unmarried fellow when the Japanese flew in and attacked our ships. His stories about that Sunday were so vivid that I almost believed I could hear the president's voice over the crackle of the radio as he addressed the nation. My dad enlisted in the Army the very next day. In December of 1944, he found himself stuck right smack-dab in the middle of the Ardennes Offensive. . . ."

Eastern Belgium
December 1944

Never could Irving Chilton remember being so miserable. Not last month when he'd come as near as ever to being blown into fragments by a mine that had taken the legs and life of the soldier ahead of him. Not in October when a barrage of German artillery shells had reduced him to a quivering, crying excuse of a GI in his foxhole. Not even when he was eight and a half years old and recovering from a vicious mauling by a stray dog.

A burst of machine-gun fire sounded somewhere outside, followed by the sound of laughter. A few minutes later, a window shattered. More laughter. Night had fallen in this little Belgian village where he was trapped, where earlier his American platoon and several civilians had been taken prisoners of war. At dusk they had been forced into a snowpacked courtyard by Germans wearing SS insignias on their caps, many of them decorated with a death's-head.

A German officer had come to stand before them, his icy gaze flicking over the shivering cluster of prisoners. "The First SS Panzer Division wishes you a very happy Christmas," he had called out in mocking tones before stepping away.

The men who had stormed the village on this day were not tired, second-rate German soldiers. When Hitler had launched his massive counterattack in mid-December, which had caught the Allies unawares, he did so with the might of three German armies. These troops had the appearance of lean, hard killers who had been seasoned at the Russian front. Their motto, decreed by Hitler, was to show no human inhibitions.

And they did not.

Upon the officer's order, they opened fire, ruthlessly cutting down their herded prisoners. Irving was pushed to the ground by the falling bodies in front of him. He lay there, scarcely breathing, while the SS walked around the bodies, pumping additional bullets into any that showed signs of life. Finally, after slaking their thirst for blood and amusement, the enemy left the victims where they had fallen and went off to seek the finest food and lodging the village could supply.

When at last he dared to move, Irving cautiously emerged from the pile of crumpled, bleeding bodies. Crouching low, he made his way down a dark, narrow street littered with rubble and entered an abandoned house. *Why am I here?* he cried out in his spirit, sinking to the floor. Everything was so horribly unreal, yet so horribly real. *Where are You, God? Why did You allow all these people to be murdered and leave me alive? Why spare me if I'm only to be killed in the morning?*

Cold to the bone, he curled up on his side, his back to the wall. No windows remained in this small house, and the winter wind took no pity upon him. How long he lay in the darkness he did not know, but the sound of a woman's scream roused him. Coarse male laughter ensued, followed by the woman's tearful pleading. Again she cried for help, but this time she was silenced in mid-scream. Scuffling noises and piteous whimpering carried through the window opening, replacing Irving's frozen misery with burning, righteous outrage.

Irving crept out the doorway, hugging the face of the building. Yellow light spilled from windows far down the street, revealing the scene of the violation, perhaps twenty-five yards distant. Two soldiers—one standing and one on hands and knees—looked down on a prone figure. Quickly Irving's mind sorted through his options while he inched closer to the street corner ahead, taking care not to stumble while picking his way through the darkest of the shadows. His weapons had been stripped from him upon capture, leaving him without so much as his trench knife.

Speed and silence were necessary to rescue the woman without drawing attention from other German troops. Irving seized a weapon that was plentifully at hand: a brick. Intent upon their wicked sport, the soldiers were not aware of his approach.

And as luck would have it, neither man was wearing a helmet.

Irving drew back the brick and struck the head of the man who was standing. He went down with a soft grunt. Neither did the second man know what hit him as he collapsed upon the woman. With grim efficiency, Irving pulled the man away by the neck and made certain he would not trouble them again. There was no need to do so with the first man. From both emanated the pungent fumes of an evening spent imbibing.

"Shhh," he whispered to the woman, who had started to crawl away, weeping quietly. "I am American." Keeping his eyes averted, he urged her to cover herself and prepare to escape.

A whispered torrent of French greeted his ears as he removed coats, weapons, rations, and canteens from the Germans' bodies. One at a time he pulled the men into the nearest doorway. The silhouette of an open trapdoor was a welcome sight, and he maneuvered both bodies through the opening, where they fell with dull thumps to the cellar floor below.

When Irving finished, the woman was standing,

already holding most of the supplies. From the illuminated houses ahead carried the sounds of revelry. He picked up the remaining provisions and spoke into her ear. "Come with me. We can't stay here."

They started off in the direction from which he had come, covering only a few yards before a voice called out in German. Plaintive, revealing the owner's drunkenness, the voice called first for Hartmann, then for Vogt. A figure appeared from the cross street, stood for a minute or more in the center of the road, then staggered on, continuing to call his comrades' names. The two had been posted as guards, Irving surmised. At some point, the inebriation of the enemy troops notwithstanding, they would be missed.

The woman tugged at his arm and said something unintelligible, pointing to a building across the street. He followed as she quickly crossed the ice-rutted road and entered a building that had sustained significant artillery damage. The woman clearly knew her way, leading through one room and into another, then down into a vegetable cellar.

As Irving descended the wobbly wooden treads into musty blackness, he felt a moment of claustrophobia grip him. He pulled the door shut behind them, forcing from his mind the notion that he and the woman were trading one grisly fate for another.

"Never give up hope, Irving," his mother had often told him. *"Just when you think things are going to turn out one way, they turn out another. That's God's way."*

Lorna Mae Chilton had spoken from experience. A war widow with two young daughters, she could not have foreseen the great love that would blossom with her late husband's younger brother. Despite the shadow of tragedy, her marriage to Irving's father was one of extraordinary happiness.

The only real adversity to visit their family during Irving's lifetime had been caused by the stray dog that attacked his sister Mabel. Irving was only eight—six years younger than his sister. Hearing Mabel's screams, he rushed to her and succeeded in turning the focus of the animal's attack. Mabel sustained bites to her arms and lower limbs, but the dog pulled Irving down and savaged one side of his face before a neighbor man came with a shovel and took care of things.

The pain caused by the wound and subsequent operations was nothing compared to the suffering Irving endured in the years afterward. Though his true friends were loyal, they could not shield him from the stares of others, the giggles, the cruel comments. And no matter how he might pine for a young woman with whom he could share his life, he did not believe marriage was in his future.

He'd welcomed a new beginning as a soldier. Because his body was strong and he was not afraid to take chances, he had quickly earned the respect of his lieutenant and platoon mates. Much to his surprise, they didn't care what his face looked like, only that he was trustworthy and could fight. While the war was horrible in more ways than Irving could count, life in the Army gave him an odd sense of liberation that he had not experienced since early childhood.

But not now. Not near a woman. Even in the dark, he was aware of the thick scar that twisted the left side of his face.

"Merci, monsieur." The woman spoke softly into the darkness, following her thanks with several sentences he didn't understand. Her voice grew tearful

and she sniffled. He heard her put down the items she carried, then settle to the floor herself.

"I'm sorry," he replied awkwardly. "I don't speak French."

"I . . . no speak *anglais.*"

His sympathy for her grew as she sniffled again in an effort to disguise her tears. What terror and humiliation she must have experienced he could not imagine, and he felt his heart tug painfully for want of comforting her. Yet with the barriers posed by language, darkness, and fear, he dared not even pat her hand.

Instead he assessed their quarters. He found a lantern hanging from a hook on the wall, but would not gamble with their lives by lighting it.

At least it was warmer here than outside. With the coats they had taken from the Germans, they might have some success warding off the chill. Irving opened one of the German ration packs and offered the woman some crackers and dried fruit. Though he didn't feel hungry, he had learned the lesson of eating regularly to maintain energy. While he chewed the cold, tasteless fare, he felt for the canteens and handed one to the woman.

Again she thanked him in her fluid, lilting tongue.

He sighed, wishing he could understand her. He did not possess a knack for picking up languages like some of the soldiers he knew. She was a local, he presumed, young and pretty enough to be deemed by the enemy to be of greater use alive than dead, at least for the time being. With helpless frustration, he realized that he could not ask her anything . . . who she was, how badly she was hurt, where they were, where they might be able to flee.

Irving sat down beside her, careful to leave a distance between them. They ate in silence—he with the uneasy awareness of their uncertain position; she no doubt reflecting on much more. If only he could tell her how sorry he was for not reaching her sooner, for not defending her from the cruelty she had suffered.

He heard her swallow a drink, followed by the soft clinking of the chain against the side of the canteen as she replaced the lid. If he were her, he would have great difficulty touching anything that had belonged to those two soldiers. But perhaps she, too, realized that survival depended on maintaining physical strength.

"My name is Irving Chilton," he said with exaggerated slowness, keeping his voice low. "Irving Chilton."

"Irving Chilton," she repeated in a way that would have been delightful if not for their present predicament. "Solange Nadal," she responded. *"Je suis Solange Nadal."*

"I'm pleased to meet you, *Madame* Nadal."

"C'est mademoiselle."

"Mademoiselle."

She said something, her words trailing off in a question.

"I'm sorry, *mademoiselle,*" Irving finally said. "I don't understand."

A dainty sigh left her, as if she, too, were frustrated by their inability to communicate.

"We should try and get some rest," he said, tucking the German coat snugly around himself. "Good night, Miss Nadal. *Bonne nuit.* God bless you."

"Gott?" After using the German word for God, she took in a sharp breath and resumed speaking.

Oh, Monsieur Chilton and *Dieu* were all he understood for certain, but her excitement at his having spoken God's name was definite. Soon it was evident that she was praying, her whispers breaking into soft sobs. It suddenly struck him that she might have sustained more tragedy this day. Had she lost family and friends in the sundown massacre? His heart went out to her yet again, and he interceded silently on her behalf.

With her hushed *amen,* she fell quiet. Before closing his eyes, he pulled the guns and ammunition near, placing one of the knives beneath his coat. With one ear cocked, listening for trouble, he was finally able to drift into an uneasy sleep. Terrifying visions visited him, as did delayed, piercing grief for his comrades who had been mown down. It was almost as if he were living the events of the day all over again. The sights, the sounds . . .

Irving awoke with a jerk. The shooting and artillery fire weren't in his dreams; they were occurring above. Wan daylight filtered through the cracks between the floorboards above them, enabling him to make out his surroundings. The cellar was small, approximately nine feet by seven feet.

Empty, grimy shelves lined two walls. A burlap bag containing what felt like a few turnips lay in one corner. Otherwise the space was barren. The war, a hard winter, and the threat of German occupation had taken their toll on this family's stores. Suddenly remembering the woman, he turned and saw that she was awake also.

He had not been able to see her clearly the night before, but this morning he was startled by her loveliness, though it was marred by the livid bruise across her cheekbone. Her hair and eyes were dark, with graceful brows. She appeared younger than his nineteen years, and rage rose within him again at the thought of the violation to which she had been subjected.

Irving saw that she had taken one of the German rifles and now held it trained on the top of the stairs. He nodded in approval while he wondered about the battle outside. Were the Americans attacking, or were the Germans continuing to pillage what had been a charming little community? An artillery shell hit nearby, its concussion shaking the earth and causing something heavy—part of a wall?—to thunder to the floor above.

While dirt and dust sifted over them, Solange buried her face beneath the coat. Irving covered his mouth and nose, stifling the urge to cough or sneeze. A machine-gun burst sounded somewhere near, accompanied by a metallic shower of empty casings. Irving felt his heart slam hard against his ribs when he heard footsteps and German voices over their heads.

It was unnecessary to warn Solange of the need for absolute silence; her wide eyes and stricken expression conveyed her grasp of the situation. He pointed first to her, then to himself, before putting his hands together and bowing his head in a pantomime of prayer. She nodded, made the sign of the cross, and began to pray, her lips moving in silent supplication.

Time stretched into what seemed like an eternity. Because his watch had been confiscated along with his weapons, he had no idea of the hour. As the sounds of battle continued, he deduced that there were two German soldiers above, stationed to shoot from the front of this particular building.

If that were the case, perhaps the Allies were indeed trying to force the enemy out of this village.

Though he beseeched the Lord for the Allies' swift success, the engagement went on and on. Not daring to change position, he and Solange sat as still as statues in their chilly hiding place that whole day through. Just as Irving's physical discomforts were growing too great to ignore any longer, the noise stopped. From above came the sounds of heavy footsteps, then nothing.

The bit of gray light they had been granted was fast fading when Irving stood, his cramped muscles protesting at the movement. Quietly he climbed a few steps and listened carefully at the trapdoor. From outside he again heard voices speaking German. Shaking his head, he climbed back down.

"We can't leave," he whispered. "The Germans are still outside."

Solange may not have understood his words, but she knew their meaning. In the near dark, he saw her nod. Fighting the desperate feeling of being trapped, he took fresh stock of their situation. They were armed, but the fact that they remained behind enemy lines greatly diminished that advantage. If they rationed their food and water carefully, they might have enough to last another day, two at best.

A most pressing need for him, and undoubtedly for Solange, was elimination. Using a cup that fit around the bottom of a canteen, he dug a primitive latrine in the corner. They took turns, and he heard Solange draw in several agonized breaths.

Irving busied himself opening another pack of rations, moved with pity and feeling utterly useless. If only there were another woman here to speak to her, to offer comfort and whatever first aid might be necessary. It was small consolation that her body would eventually heal from its injuries if her heart and spirit never did.

They ate in silence, having resumed their sitting positions against the wall. Total darkness had wrapped itself around them once again, and his hopes for a quiet night were shattered when the shrieking sounds of shelling began once again.

"Non," Solange breathed from beside him, her words ending in a strangled sob.

"The Lord *Gott . . . Dieu . . . Nôtre Père . . .* knows our plight, *Mademoiselle* Nadal." It was silly to reassure her with words she could not understand, but perhaps she might feel comfort in his voice. "If He knows when the sparrow falls from flight, then He certainly knows where we are. All my life, my mother has told me to never give up hope. My father reminded me to keep short accounts, because a man never knows when his final day on earth will be. What I'm trying to say . . . well, somewhere in all that . . . is that maybe we'll die here. Maybe we won't. The Germans can take our lives, but they can't take our souls. Because of Christ, *mademoiselle,* we have the hope of heaven. Who could comprehend the suffering the Son of God endured to return to His kingdom? And all of it for our benefit. If we wish to follow Him there, we must also follow in the way of suffering."

Irving's heart swelled with fierce tenderness when she reached for his hand. He had enlisted in the Army with the ideals of helping to defend people against the onslaught of an enemy who would oppress them. But in Solange Nadal, his principles had been lifted to another plane. The woman beside him was not a nameless victim but a living, frightened, wounded soul who had, through some twist of fate, been given to him for safeguarding.

"I promise to protect you, *Mademoiselle* Nadal,"

he vowed, cupping her hand in his, "so long as I have life and limb to do so."

A blast nearby rattled the stairs and sent her into his arms. Dirt rained down on them, and he wondered if it was foolishness to remain in a cellar that could so easily entomb them. The alternatives, however, were no better. To climb above ground would put them amidst heavy fire, and they surely would be cut down if they tried to escape. Surrender, he knew, would mean torture or death.

For now, they were utterly reliant on the mercy of God.

While Irving prayed as a man who knew his life depended on it, a new sound chilled his blood. Only last summer, the Germans had unleashed their enormous Royal Tiger tanks. A Tiger's size alone was terrifying to behold—twice as large as a 34-ton U.S. Sherman tank. The snarl of its 700-horsepower engine was distinctive as was the way its massive weight made the earth tremble.

The powerful vibrations that traveled through the ground at this moment were unmistakable, and despair threatened to choke him as he realized panzer reinforcements had rolled in to bolster the

Germans' position. He and Solange were never going to get out of this cellar alive.

"Königstiger." She spoke the German word for the monstrous tank and shuddered against him.

"Oui," he confirmed.

The night was awful to endure, made worse by a new wave of bombing from the air. Any moment might bring a hit that snuffed out their lives or buried them alive. Irving found himself lightheaded at times from holding his breath. Yet Solange's warm presence beside him brought a certain comfort, and he thanked God for the gift of her companionship in the midst of this horror.

Daylight brought no slowing of the battle. If anything, it intensified. Irving opened the last of the rations and offered them to Solange. She took a small amount and pushed the rest toward him. He tried again, but she shook her head, motioning for him to eat the remainder.

While the hours passed, he tried imagining what was happening outside. From the sound of things, the Allies persisted in their offensive while the Germans were just as determined to hold the ground they had seized. One strike brought the wooden shelves clattering down upon them. Just in time, he raised his arms to protect Solange from being struck.

At times their predicament seemed dreamlike; at others, all too real. As the second day passed into night, Irving wondered how much longer they could go on. They had been in this cellar for more than forty-eight hours now, and their rations and water were gone. His lips felt like the bottom of a dried-up creek bed, and his tongue stuck to the roof of his mouth.

Neither of them found the solace of sleep that night, and when the third morning broke, he was alarmed by Solange's appearance. Her eyes had sunken into their sockets, and her movements were listless. The fighting sounded fainter now, farther away. If he could get some ice or snow for hydration, perhaps that would help revive her.

When he stood, he noticed his own weakness. After signaling his intent to go above, he slung a rifle over his shoulder and climbed the stairs. When at first the trapdoor would not budge, he imagined a whole wall of the house lying atop it. But he pushed again, this time with all his might, and heard whatever was across the opening slide away.

The brightness was painful and blinding. As his eyes began to adjust, he saw that the house under which they had taken refuge was a ruin. Most of the roof was gone, and the front wall facing the street was nonexistent. How they had managed to escape harm had to be a miracle, for a huge crater pocked the street. The buildings directly across from them were gone.

Seeing no movement in the vicinity, Irving made his way to a pile of dirty, packed snow and began to scoop at it with the canteen cup. The day was cold and clear, its chill reviving his vigor. Intent on his task, he failed to notice the pair of soldiers who rounded the corner.

"Hands in the air," a voice commanded, first in poorly accented German, then in English, with the inflection of the American Midwest.

American!

The second GI shouldered his M1 rifle. "Surrender, or I'll be more than happy to shoot."

With slow, deliberate movements, Irving let go of the cup and laid down the gun. He raised his hands above his head, his joy tempered by the knowledge that his coat and firearm were of German issue. If these soldiers had seen the carnage of the village courtyard, they might be more inclined to pull their triggers than to take prisoners. "Private Irving Chilton, 424th, Second Platoon, Delta Company. Three days ago we were surrounded."

"Yeah? How do we know you're not a Kraut?"

"Open the coat," Irving suggested, keeping his hands in the air as the first man approached. "You'll see my uniform underneath."

"What's the capital of Idaho?" the second man called, not relaxing his stance.

"Ah . . . Boise," replied Irving.

"Kentucky?"

"Frankfort."

"Who's Mickey Mouse's girlfriend?" questioned the first soldier, his eyes hard, parting the front of Irving's coat with his rifle barrel.

"Minnie Mouse." Irving tried to remain calm, realizing the GIs had to be sure he was who he claimed to be. Lately it had been discovered that teams of German spies, speaking flawless English, had been sent behind Allied lines for the purpose of sabotage.

"Who won the 1939 World Series?"

Irving took a deep breath. "New York Yankees walloped the Cincinnati Reds in four games. The first and second were at Yankee Stadium, where it was the Yankees over the Reds, 2-1 and 4-0. Game three was at Crosley Field in Cincinnati. DiMaggio and Dickey each hit homers, and Keller hit two—"

"All right, all right," the first soldier said, his tense expression easing into a rueful grin. He pulled back his rifle and saluted. "Private Jim Nelson, 506th Parachute Infantry, 101st Airborne. You must have a tale to tell, Chilton. You wounded?"

"No, but the local I've been holed up with is going to need some attention."

"Where is he?"

"She," Irving corrected, leading them to the cellar door. "*Mademoiselle,* the Americans are here," he called down, fearing she might panic and fire the weapon she held.

Private Nelson added his own greeting in

French. *"Venez, mademoiselle! Venez! Vous pouvez sortir maintenant!"*

Nelson received a grateful, tearful reply to his greeting. But before either of them could descend into the cellar to assist her, Solange stood on unsteady legs and climbed toward them. Irving extended his arm, nearly overcome by a rush of emotion when she gripped his hand and stepped out of the opening.

They had survived. They were free.

In the daylight, Solange's bruised cheekbone contrasted starkly with her smooth complexion. She was as covered with grime as he was, but even so, her beauty was apparent. Nothing could have astounded him more than when she put her hands up to his scarred face and wept as she spoke to him in her native language. When she concluded, she wiped her eyes, turned toward the French-speaking private, and said something to him.

Nodding, Private Nelson cleared his throat and looked down at his feet for a moment. "Her parents and brother were killed three days ago. At first she wished she could die too, but she says your bravery and decency gave her the courage to continue living. She believes God sent you to rescue her and show her the kindness that you did. For this, she will give thanks every day, and she promises to pray faithfully for you."

Irving was aware of Solange's solemn gaze upon him while Private Nelson translated. His face burned where she had touched him—touched his scar. Why had she done that? Why wasn't she repulsed by its appearance, as the girls in his hometown had been? A peculiar trembling began inside him, and he found it hard to take a breath.

She said something else to the private, her words earnest, then trailing off to a hush.

"She wonders if you will one day come back. She says—" here Nelson paused, then grinned—"she says she hopes you might."

"What does she think of my face?" Irving blurted out, acutely aware of the thick, twisted scar on his cheek.

He watched Private Nelson examine his disfigurement before translating the question. A sweet, sad smile curved Solange's lips as she replied.

Nelson nodded. "She says that many people have scars. Some are on the outside for all to see, but others, no less painful, are hidden deep inside a soul. She says that both of you understand what it means to bear a painful wound."

Irving swallowed hard as he gazed into Solange's bottomless, dark brown eyes. "Tell her I will come back."

And he did, after the German surrender early that May. In the warmth of a midsummer afternoon, he returned to her village and proposed marriage. That he found her with child made no difference to him. Their fledgling relationship quickly bloomed into a marriage of true and abiding love, blessed richly with the graces of fidelity, peace, and great devotion.

Meg had rarely seen her husband cry. When his father died in 1980, he had wept. At the funeral of his mother, the beautiful Solange, Dan had cried openly. Now, recalling the story of Irving Chilton's bravery, his willingness to sacrifice his life, and his love for the Frenchwoman who had been brutally violated, Dan brushed the tears from his cheeks.

Meg sniffled and leaned forward to kiss the damp skin of the man she loved so dearly. "I had no idea," she whispered.

"That's because it never mattered to Dad that another man had fathered Jake," Dan said in a low voice. "He treated both of his sons exactly the same—expected just as much from each of us and loved us with the same strength. He always introduced us as 'my best boys.' We were his 'rascals,' you know. He used to say, 'You boys make me proud to be a father.' And we believed him."

"Oh, Dan, what a wonderful man."

"He loved her, you know. He loved my mother so much."

"Enough to do the right thing," she said.

Meg reached for another tissue and blew her nose. Her husband's large, work-worn fingers slid through hers as she lifted her eyes toward the window. The afternoon sun streamed through the clean glass and lit up the array of memorabilia on her desk—medals, old letters, yellowed newspaper clippings, official documents. This legacy, this collection of mementos of the Chilton family, was really all about one thing: love.

Through their courage and boldness, the Chiltons had shown the real meaning of that word. True love meant being willing to sacrifice everything—to surrender all hopes of security, comfort, and peace . . . to give up safety and the promise of a profitable future with family and work . . . to lay down even one's own life.

Meg squeezed her husband's hands. "Dan, I have to go now."

His expression sobered. "Go where?"

"Out."

"You okay, honey?"

She let out a deep breath. "I'm fine. Now . . . I'm all right."

Propelled by the same Spirit that had driven Tyler from the house, Meg raced down the stairs, her tennis shoes taking them in double time. Grabbing her purse and keys, she flew through the kitchen and out the back door. The screen door banged shut behind her as she slid into her car and started the engine.

In minutes she was entering the congested part of downtown. She drove past the courthouse in the center square and headed toward the Dairy Queen. As she pulled into a parking space in front of the military recruiting office next door, she spotted Tyler's truck three places down. He had climbed out and was reaching to push open the recruiter's door.

"Tyler! Tyler, wait!" Meg called.

As she jumped out of her car, her son looked back in surprise. "Mom?"

"Wait, Tyler. Wait a minute, please!"

He lowered his hand. "Mom, I've been sitting here praying about this, and I'm—"

"It's okay, Tyler. Really." She gestured to a wooden bench in front of the ice-cream shop. "Would you sit with me for just a minute?"

He cast a look at the recruiting office. "Uh . . . okay. I guess so."

Joining his mother, he walked beside her to the bench. "Tyler, I'm sorry to interrupt like this, but I need to talk to you."

"Mom, we already—"

"It's all right, honey," she said as they sat down. "This won't take but a minute."

Reaching out, Meg laid her hand on her son's back. She could feel the warmth of his skin beneath his T-shirt, the precious heat of life that throbbed in his veins. The curve of his shoulder beneath her palm reminded Meg of his birth, his tiny body pushing through the cocoon of her womb and emerging into the light and air and freedom of the wide world.

"Go," she said softly. "Go, my son, Tyler John Chilton, into your new life. I bless you with my whole heart. I honor your decision to do the will of God, and I make a covenant now to pray for you and support you in all you do throughout your future years on this earth. 'May the Lord bless you and protect you. May the Lord smile on you and be gracious to you,' Tyler Chilton. 'May the Lord show you His favor and give you His peace.' Amen."

Leaning forward, Meg pressed her lips to her

son's forehead. But as she straightened, Tyler wrapped his arms around her. "Thanks, Mom," he said against her ear. "I love you."

"I love you too, honey." Then she pulled back and set him away from her. Looking across at the glass door of the recruiter's office, she drew a deep breath and said, "Okay, Uncle Sam, he's all yours."

Before her son could see her tears, Meg rose from the bench and strode back to her car.

Meg stood beside her husband and watched from a discreet distance as Tyler conversed with the other recruits who had arrived at the airport. Jake and Martha waited nearby, their hands around fortifying cups of coffee and their tissues at the ready.

"He looks little," Meg said in a low voice. "I think it must be that haircut."

"I was just thinking how grown-up he looks," Dan returned. "Like an adult."

She gave a laugh. "To me, he seems like a small boy on his way to kindergarten. Aren't parents weird?"

"Pretty weird," Dan agreed. "I keep thinking how God must have felt sending His only Son down to earth to suffer and die for us. Just awful, I'd imagine."

"A righteous king in all His glory," she said, "forced into the flesh of a newborn baby."

"Yeah, with a couple of poor, uneducated human parents to raise Him, teach Him, and protect Him. It's hard to send Tyler off to basic training. But boot camp is nothing compared to the destiny that Jesus faced."

"God must love us so much."

"More than we can even imagine." Dan let out a breath. "And Tyler's doing what he believes is God's will. That's the main thing. We have to remember this, Meg. No matter where they send him."

As Dan spoke these words, Tyler left his group and walked toward them. "Well, they're going to take us back into the military waiting area. We'll board the plane from there."

Meg swallowed hard. So this was it. The moment she had been dreading. As Uncle Jake and Aunt Martha hugged Tyler, she drew a small packet from her purse.

"Be careful, Son," Dan said, embracing the boy

in a rough hug. "You make me proud to be a father."

"Thanks, Dad." Tyler chucked his father on the arm. "You're the best."

Turning to his mother, he suddenly threw his arms around her, picked her up, and squeezed her so tight the air whooshed from her lungs. She let out a little squeal as he set her down again and gave her a brisk peck on the cheek.

"Don't cry, Mom," he said, holding out a warning finger. "This is the right thing."

She nodded. "Here," she whispered, pressing the packet into his hands. "It's the journal I kept, and a copy of the chart."

"The great-great-greats?"

"All of 'em."

Tyler grinned. "I figured you were going to foist them off on me sooner or later."

"Read their stories. You'll understand why you had to do this."

"I already understand." His pointed finger jabbed toward heaven. "Gotta do what you gotta do."

"Have fun, Tyler," Meg said as he turned to go. "I love you."

"I love you too. All you guys. Be good!"

With a casual saunter, he rejoined the other young recruits. A uniformed man with snowy white hair beckoned, and they followed him down a hall and around a corner, vanishing from sight.

As Meg stood there, feeling suddenly alone and cold, she thought of the journal in Tyler's hand—the solid, physical record of the brave men and women whose lifeblood flowed through her son's veins. He might never read the words she had penned, but she felt good knowing he had it. These people—and the ancestors of every young man and woman who had walked down that hall moments ago—had paved the path to the freedom and blessing that made America such a great nation.

Now Tyler Chilton was joining their ranks.

Dan stepped up beside his wife, slipped his arm around her, and held her close. Though it was the most difficult thing she had ever done, Meg knew an abiding peace as she rested her head on her husband's strong shoulder. *Dear God*, she lifted up in the silence of the airport. *Keep my loved one safe. Nevertheless, not my will but Yours be done.*

About the Authors

CATHERINE PALMER's first book was published in 1988, and since then she has published more than thirty books. Total sales of her novels number more than one million copies.

Catherine's novels *The Happy Room* and *A Dangerous Silence* are CBA best-sellers, and her HeartQuest book *A Touch of Betrayal* won the 2001 Christy Award (Romance category). Her novella "Under His Wings," which appears in the anthology *A Victorian Christmas Cottage,* was named Northern Lights Best Novella of 1999 (Historical category) by Midwest Fiction Writers. Her numerous other awards include Best Historical Romance, Best Contemporary Romance, Best of Romance from the Southwest Writers Workshop, Most Exotic Historical Romance Novel from *Romantic Times* magazine, and Best Historical Romance Novel from Romance Writers of the Panhandle.

Catherine lives in Missouri with her husband, Tim, and sons, Geoffrey and Andrei. She has degrees from Baylor University and Southwest Baptist University.

PEGGY STOKS lives in Minnesota with her husband and three children. A former registered nurse, she now enjoys working from home. Writing fiction gives her the opportunity to blend her faith in God, her love of history, and her knowledge of health, illness, and injury.

In the future, Peggy hopes to continue crafting rich and satisfying novels that weave together timeless truths about people, faith, and God. It is her most fervent hope that her work gives readers food for thought and inspires them to grow in holiness. Peggy's previous books include *Olivia's Touch, Romy's Walk, Elena's Song,* and *A Victorian Christmas Collection.*

BOOKS BY BEST-SELLING AUTHOR
CATHERINE PALMER

NEARLY 1 MILLION CAREER SALES!

Visit www.movingfiction.net

Turn the page for an exciting preview of

A VICTORIAN ROSE

a very special gift book by Catherine Palmer

(ISBN 0-8423-1957-3)

Available now from Tyndale House Publishers

Clemma seated herself at a table upon which she had gathered a collection of late autumn flora—chrysanthemums, asters, rose hips, and ears of ripe wheat. Although she had planned to paint each month's flowers at the height of their bloom, in midsummer she had fallen behind schedule. Now the mums were past their prime, and the asters had begun to droop. She must get them into water immediately or her entire project was likely to wilt as well.

"Will you stay to tea, Mr. Hedgley?" she asked as she began stripping away dead leaves. "I expect it will be brought down from the great house at any moment. You are more than welcome to join me."

"Nay, but thank ye, Mrs. Laird, for I must be gettin' back to me own cottage lest Mrs. 'edgley give me a piece of 'er mind. Farewell, then."

"Good afternoon, Mr. Hedgley."

Clemma hardly noticed the old man as he moved down the path inside the conservatory. Absorbed in arranging the asters in a vase, she felt a flutter of panic in her stomach. This exhibition of her art was the most important thing to happen to her in many years, and she was determined to make it a success.

Raised near the little Yorkshire town of Otley, she had always dreamed of sailing the seven seas, riding horseback across the American frontier, bowing before Indian maharajas, and finding the source of the Nile. But at her father's insistence, she had followed the example of her three elder sisters and married young. It was a blessed union, for not only had Clemma loved Thomas Laird, but marrying him had made her the mistress of a fine manor and the wife of a wealthy man. Not a full year into the marriage, however, their grand home was struck by lightning. It caught fire and burned to the ground. Thomas perished in the blaze.

Clemma, who was badly injured, had deeply mourned the death of her young husband. She moved back to the family home of Brooking House to recover, and slowly she assumed full care for her aging parents. Somehow, in the years that drifted by, her dreams of adventure and passion faded. She took lessons in the art school housed at nearby Longley Park, and she spent most of her time painting flowers inside the great conservatory. Now, at thirty-two, she knew she would never remarry, and she was far too settled to explore Africa or sail away to India. She was, she realized, a bit dull.

Gazing at the chrysanthemums she had placed in the vase with the asters, she leaned her elbows on the table and rested her chin in her hands. Dull. Dispirited. Boring. How had she withered away to such a pale vestige of her former self? How had she let herself become so . . .

"No!" she cried out, slapping her hands down on the table and pushing herself up. She would not succumb to this spirit of defeat that assailed her. Grasping a stick of charcoal, she turned to her easel and began to sketch the outline of the simple glass vase. God had blessed her with a good life, and she was a happy woman. She needed nothing, no one.

"Excuse me, miss!"

The voice came from the far end of the conservatory. It was the footman with the tea.

"Put it on the small table in the niche near the palm trees," Clemma called. "I do hope you warmed the milk this time."

"I beg your pardon?"

She glanced around the frame of her canvas at the footman. Tall and broad shouldered, he stared at her with icy blue eyes. Why was he not wearing his livery? Clemma wondered as she stepped out from behind the easel. And where was the tea tray?

"Did you say something about milk?" he asked, starting down the path toward her. She could see now that the man was not as young as she first had supposed, for his dark brown hair was threaded with silver, and subtle lines softened the outer corners of his eyes. Moreover, he did not look much like a footman. Wearing a long black frock coat with velvet cuffs, he sported an embroidered waistcoat of indigo blue and a silk cravat.

"Milk," she repeated, feeling a little off balance. "Indeed, I thought you had come about the tea."

"No . . . oranges, to be exact. Oranges and lemons."

"Oranges?" Her focus darted to the double rows of orange trees hanging heavy with fruit. "What can you mean, sir?"

"I wish to purchase a dozen oranges. I should be pleased to take several lemons as well. And some limes, if you have them."

"Goodness, I mistook you for the footman!" she said, feeling a flush of heat pour into her cheeks. "Not that you resemble a servant, of course, for you are clearly a gentleman, and . . . that is . . . we normally do not sell the fruit grown in the conservatory . . . sir."

A Victorian Rose

"What becomes of it?"

"The kitchens use it in providing meals for the art students who have taken residence at Longley Park."

"Am I to assume you are one of these students?"

He glanced at her easel, and Clemma felt intense gratitude that it was turned the wrong way around. For some reason, this man disconcerted her, and she was not sure why. He was certainly handsome, and he displayed the elegance and mannerisms of a gentleman. Yet he had a stilted air about him, an upright sort of stiffness that gave him the look of a mannequin in a shopwindow. It was as though he were not quite real, not completely human.

"No, sir," she said. "My student days are long behind me."

"Then you are the proprietress of the conservatory?"

"Indeed, no, for all the gardening at Longley Park is administered by Mr. Hedgley."

His dark eyebrows lifted. "Then may I ask who gives you the authority to refuse my request?"

Though the question was placed with civility, Clemma read the tinge of disdain it contained. But she had a ready answer.

"I am Clementine Laird, sir. My sister, Mrs. Ivy Richmond, is mistress of Longley."

"And this relationship gives you leave to make decisions regarding its citrus fruits?"

She looked to see if he were joking, but she recognized

no hint of levity in his eyes. "My sister and her husband are away in India," she said. "But . . . no . . . I am not exactly in charge of making decisions here, for that would fall to Mr. Thompson, the family's solicitor. Or perhaps Mr. Wiggins, the butler, is responsible . . . though more rightly it might be the housekeeper, Mrs. Gold, for she is . . ." She paused and frowned. "At any rate, you may not purchase fruit from the conservatory. I am sorry."

Ducking behind her easel, she focused on her sketch of the vase as she hoped mightily that the man would go away. Instead, she heard again the sound of his footsteps approaching. Fearful lest he might peek at her drawing— which suddenly seemed poorly done indeed—Clemma rounded the easel and faced him.

"Sir, may I be so bold as to know your name?" she said. "I believe I may be compelled to report this incident of trespassing to the constable in Otley."

To her surprise, the man paled and took a step backward. "I beg you, do no such thing, Miss Laird. I come with no ill intent."

"Then who are you, and why must you continue to insist upon purchasing lemons and oranges?"

"I am a physician." He hesitated a moment. "My name is Paul Baine."

As he spoke those words, Clemma felt her blood plummet to her knees. "Dr. Baine?" she repeated numbly.

"Is my name familiar to you?"

"Indeed, it is, sir." Trying to regain her composure, Clemma extended the stick of charcoal toward him, as if it were a sword that might protect her. From the earliest days of her youth, she had heard tales of the man who lived at Nasmyth Manor, the darkly shuttered house on a wind-swept fell some distance from the village of Otley. Dr. Baine kept himself and his practices hidden away—and it was well he did so, for had he flaunted his evils, the town would have driven him off.

It was rumored that women burdened with unwanted pregnancies slipped through the mists of night to knock on the door of Nasmyth Manor. In a day or two, they returned to their cottages, and not a word was spoken of what had taken place at the hands of Dr. Baine.

Not only did the man perform these unspeakable acts, but he also saw patients who had contracted diseases from their profligate activities. It was rumored that sailors came from Scarborough Harbour and the coastal cities of Hull, Whitby, and Filey to be treated with a special cure that Dr. Baine had developed. The fallen women who consorted with these men came, too, as did villagers who had ventured to Leeds for an evening of revelry and had returned with more than they had bargained for. The man who stood before Clemma had enriched himself by these most repulsive means. He was a fiend.

"Begone!" she cried, thrusting the charcoal stick at him. "Begone from this place, or I shall . . . I shall . . ."

"You need not fear me, Miss Laird—"

"I do not fear you—I revile you! Go away from here at once. As a Christian, I find that the very sight of you sickens me!"

A strange light flickered in his eyes. "You are a Christian. Of course." He shrugged his shoulders. "Nevertheless, I must have the citrus fruits, madam."

"Never. I would not allow you the smallest crumb from my table, let alone permit you to feast upon these beautiful oranges from my sister's hall."

"I do not want them for myself."

"No? And why should I believe anything you say?"

"Why should I believe anything you say? We are strangers, are we not? What you appear to know of me is only by rumor and reputation. I know you only by what you have chosen to reveal about yourself, Miss Laird."

"Mrs. Laird, if you please. I am a widow. And if you question my truthfulness, I shall . . . I shall . . ."

"You are not very good at making threats, Mrs. Laird," he said, one corner of his elegant mouth tipping up. "Madam, I have very politely approached you and begged permission to purchase fruit. It is not to be eaten by me, whom you seem to find so odious, but by someone who is in dire need of the sustenance it provides. And so I implore you, Mrs. Laird. I appeal to your Christian charity. May you please find it in your pious and devoted heart to assist one so far beneath you as my humble self?"

So saying, he fell on one knee, his arms outstretched and his head bowed.

Clemma was so stunned she hardly knew what to say. There could be no denying the depths of Dr. Baine's wickedness. Though she had never met him before, the tales of his villainous treatments had persisted so many years that they could not be anything but true. He rarely came into the village, and he never set foot in church. If he had, he would have been shunned by one and all.

Yet, this vile man had pointed out Clemma's Christian duty to act charitably. How could she refuse the fruit to one who must be in great need of its nourishment? But what if Dr. Baine planned to eat the oranges and lemons himself? What if his story were all a lie? Then she would be playing directly into his hand.

"Get up at once, sir," she said, irritated at the indecision that plagued her. Did a Christian have an obligation to help those less fortunate—no matter what? No matter if the one in need was some bedraggled creature who had chosen to end the precious life growing within her womb? No matter if the hungry soul was a pestilent seaman who had spread his filth from port to port around the world? Oh dear!

"Sir, I beg you to rise," she said again. "Your mockery disgusts me, and your posturing is insufferable."

"I shall rise only when you have permitted me to purchase oranges and lemons," he said, his head bowed. "I cannot leave this place without accomplishing my mission."

Clemma stared down at the man's bent head. His dark hair was in need of a trim, but the collar of his white shirt had been crisply starched and pressed. The fabric was very fine, she noted, and the cut of his frock coat bespoke exquisite tailoring. No doubt his coffers had been well filled by those wretched and desperate souls who came to him in their need. Of course he could charge any price for his services, for no respectable physician would undertake such unmentionable tasks. Indeed, the practice was illegal, Clemma felt sure, though no one who had made use of it would dare to testify against him. Certainly Dr. Baine was the only such doctor in this entire region of Yorkshire, and his wealth must be immeasurable.

"Five pounds," she said. "Per orange."

His head shot up. "Five pounds for a single orange? You must be mad!"

"I am not. You can afford to pay my price, and as I possess the only oranges in Yorkshire on this particular November day, you have no choice. Agree to it now, or I shall raise the price to seven pounds."

"Preposterous!" he said, rising.

"No more so than the outrageous fees you surely must charge for your despicable practices. Five pounds per orange. And I shall place your money into the offering box at church, where it may be washed clean and then put to good use ministering to the needy in the name of Jesus Christ."

The icy blue eyes narrowed. "Mrs. Laird," he snarled, "you are not a godly woman."

"Oh, yes I am!" she cried, stepping toward him. "I worship Jesus as Lord and Savior, I go to church every Sunday, I do good deeds for the poor, and I do not associate with wicked men such as yourself!"

"Five pounds, then," he said, jerking his wallet from his coat. "Fetch me an orange!"

Clemma grabbed the money he held out and set off down the path toward the orangery. Such a horrid man! He did not deserve anything good in this life. She had half a mind to throw his money back at him and run outside to call for assistance in ridding Longley Park of such a miscreant.

But in the years since her husband's death, Clemma had learned to rely on no one but God and herself. She could certainly handle Dr. Baine without any help. Eyeing the double rows of healthy trees, she selected a small, greenish fruit and plucked it from the limb. There, this sour thing would do him very well.

When she swung around, she realized he stood directly behind her on the path. "Your orange, Dr. Baine," she said, handing it to him.

"I need another." He held out a second five-pound note. "I must have it. And how much will you charge me for a lemon?"

Clemma was about to send him away with another

harsh rebuke when she recognized something in his face that startled her. He was pleading. His eyes were filled with a mixture of hope and doubt, and the set of his jaw revealed the utmost solemnity. At that moment Clemma saw the truth: He did indeed need the oranges. He needed them desperately. He would pay her outrageous prices without further complaint.

"For whom do you seek these oranges?" she asked.

He gazed down at the pathetic little fruit in his hand. "For one who must have them." Pausing a moment, he added, "I cannot say more."

Without hesitation, Clemma reached up and tugged two more oranges from the tree. Then she hurried to the edge of the small grove and pulled down a handful of lemons. "Here, take these, sir, and begone." She thrust them into his hands. "And do not come to this place again, I beg you."

"You will not take payment for the remainder of the fruit, Mrs. Laird?"

"I do not want it."

"You are good."

She lifted her head. "A moment ago you doubted my Christianity. Am I now different?"

"Perhaps. I believe all humans to be capable of change for the better. Your behavior toward me has demonstrated the validity of this notion. I am grateful." He gave her a small bow. "And now I see that your tea has arrived. I do hope the milk is warm. Good day, Mrs. Laird."

Clemma stared after him as he hurried away down the path. He passed the footman who bore a tray of tea things, and then he slipped through the glass door and was gone. Clemma started toward her easel, but the image of asters had been replaced in her thoughts by the memory of a pair of strangely beckoning blue eyes.